E. Robert Dunn

Un-Para-Llel
All Rights Reserved © 2021 - E. Robert Dunn

This book is protected under the copyright laws of the United States of America. Any reproduction or other unauthorized use of the material or artwork contained herein is prohibited without the express written permission of the copyright holder. All characters in this book are fictitious. Any resemblance to any persons, living or dead is purely coincidental.

Published by: INKPENDENT

Cover by William Green
© 2020 E. Robert Dunn /All rights reserved

MASS MARKET EDITION
Printed in the United States of America
1st Edition / Digitized: MARCH 2021

# Un – Para – Llel

By

E. Robert Dunn

https://www.facebook.com/inkpendentpublishing/

**Un-Para-Llel©**

All Rights Reserved © 2020 by E. Robert Dunn

No part of this book may be reproduced or transmitted in any form or by any means, graphic, electronic, or mechanical, including photocopying, recording, taping, or by any information storage retrieval system, without permission in writing from the publisher.

Any resemblance to actual people and events is purely coincidental.
This is a work of fiction.

ISBN: 9798595880763

Author's Note:

Gliese 667 is a triple-star system some 23.16 light years from Earth in the constellation Scorpius, lying at about 6.8 pc from Earth. All three of the stars have masses smaller than the Sun.

There is a 12th magnitude star close to the other three, but it is not gravitationally bound to the system. It is a well-studied nearby star to the Sol system. Inspired by the possibility of at least six planets orbiting the C-star, three of them within the habitable zone where liquid surface water can exist. These three planets are expected to be tidally locked, always showing the same face to their sun as they orbit.

Taking a leap of imagination, I created the Glaser star system and what might possibly orbit within as a possible parallel to Gliese. Here's hoping my projections are rational and engaging, but even more so... clairvoyant.

# Un

## OPORTO BAZARE

### CHAPTER ONE:

The dream of traveling to star systems was forged by rocketeers a century ago. From space stations constructed in planetary orbits to permanent space colonies. A predilection that had led to the evolution into a whole new species from its progenitors: *Homo cosmicus*.

Technological advances made missions to far off 'lands' possible and revolutionized life on settled planets. A steep rise, an acceleration, in the pace and invention and basic research for whole new solutions to the problems of energy, food production, health, and more occurred.

Launching probes into Space to neighboring worlds, became planet-based astronomers' sensory organs, finding some worlds were too hot, some too cold; examining other celestial bodies that happened to be flying by discovered rare metals and minerals.

All efforts yielded excellent photos and huge amounts of data on magnetic fields, on compounds, learned a great deal about the native solar system and what dangers to expect from black suns, neutron storms, radiation, and the like. Every year new knowledge added to the collective information advancing space travel to the very edge.

Venturing beyond home planet to appease curiosity. Searching for the right combination of elements in a habitable zone environment in which stable life could safely develop, grow, and subsist. For the longest time, the universe had been silent.

The initial choices for astral immigration were not the most ideal, living out lives in greenhouses; paraterraforming sections with a sample of breathable biosphere inside pressure domes, caves, and underground caverns. Every other scientific matter took a backseat to finding more accommodating habitations, the search for the holiest grail of all was on. Reaching further in cosmic terms to a stone's throw distance to the most proximal star systems to green and watery planets spawning life familiar.

Bioengineers, environmental specialists, biochemists, geologists, miners were the first to go with the exploratory branch of the military. Pathfinders.

On some rocky worlds involved seeding the atmospheres with algae, which converted the ample supplies of water, nitrogen, and carbon dioxide into organic compounds, on other planets it meant transporting low albedo material and/or planting dark plants on the polar ice caps to ensure it absorbed more heat, melted, and converted the planet to more 'livable conditions' and still on others the introduction of greenhouse gases used to create a warmer, oxygen and ozone-rich atmosphere.

Developing terra-formed roadways necessary to allow civilians to follow. The advent of advanced propulsion technologies in the understanding of dark matter, dark energy, and slipstream applied science shrunk travel time between planets from years down to months to weeks and, in some cases, days.

Those first colonist were selected for their unique balance of scientific achievement, emotional stability and pioneer resourcefulness. With a reduced round trip time and a fleet of transport ships able to relocate the first 10,000 in less than six months, and the first 80,000 in less than four years had happened.

Despite the daily drumbeat of violence and war engendered in the progenitors' DNA, the modern era had become one of the most peaceful eras in a shared history. Over the centuries, the number of fatalities killed in battle had steadily dropped as civilization evolved.

With two horrible global wars in the past century, the following was even worse. In terms of deaths per 100,000 from war, genocide, and other factors, the settled part of the galaxy was relatively calm. On the other hand, major periods of scarcity and suffering loomed.

First driven by profit, then conquest, but eventually to be of one accord, the last century saw the inhabited parts of the galaxy population grow from less than two trillion to nearly seven trillion, projected to reach nine or ten trillion within the next twenty-six years. Predicting a 70% increase in food production by then, and at least that much more energy to sustain populations.

The triple star system, Glaser 667 had been initially explored and settled by greedy prospectors aboard hybrid fusion-antimatter spaceships. Glaser 667-A and -B orbited too close to each other to have any planetary bodies that could support corporeal life recognizable as sentient, only barren worlds rich in natural resources.

667-C, a red dwarf, had six planets within its fold. Three of them small enough to be called Super Planets swung at a distance that allowed liquid water to flow on each surface. That had opened the possibility for planetary colonization. Biomarkers such as methane, methylene chlorine, nitric oxide produced by living organisms enriched in an atmosphere were identified on three planets within Glaser 667-C star group and the race was on for terra-mare development.

The first settlers had descended on innocent native hunter-gatherer peoples. To their delight, the basic bipedal model dominated not only the world of Un, but its two sister planets sharing this solar group's habitable zone. Each fully adapted for survival in three unique dominant environments: water, land, and air. Interspecies mixing of genes had commenced and been fruitful.

It was on the first habitable planet known natively as Un, that *Troodon sapiens* had evolved and thrived. Having larger relative brain size in terrestrial vertebrates through geologic time, and the energetic efficiency of an upright posture in slow-moving, bipedal animals.

The inhabitants of Un all had a large brain for their size, stereoscopic vision, resulting in a shortened facial region, reduced dentition, and the dexterity of a first digit evolved in one lineage or another. A big-brained head needed to be supported directly over the body, a short neck and vertical hominid-like posture evolved. The vertical posture meant goodbye to a tail, reduced to a stump, and the need to give birth to big-headed babies led to a broad, hominid-like pelvis. Being viviparous, equipped with a navel.

Convergences did occur in evolution. Body shapes as adaptations to a wholly aquatic lifestyle from plantigrade feet; four-toed, with nails rather than claws, with the two medial toes smaller than the lateral ones. The 'best' body plan for a big-brained tetrapod. There was no goal or endpoint to the evolutionary process.

On the planet Un, the road curving down through the hills above the fishing village of Bazare seemed deserted in the bright sunlight, a cluster of white, cubed-shaped houses, with cobblestone streets cutting down the steep slope to the sea. The town was not actually all white, the house fronts gleamed with the high glaze of colored tiles—some with small floral patterns, others with geometric designs.

The town was not empty. Every resident was down on the beach, for the pilchard fishing fleet was in.

On the Bazare Beach, too, the scene was full of pattern and color, starting with the males themselves. There was an obvious love of plaids. Patched with other plaids, all faded from sunslight and salt air and water to soft tones, but still strong and lively of line. Barefooted, the males strode briskly across the sands or sat in clusters along the beachfront street, discussing affairs of the day; on their heads, above the geometric tangle of the plaids, they wore black stocking caps.

No less colorful were their boats, pulled far up on the beach in a jumbled maze of broad curves and pointed, up-swung prows. For their small size the boats were markedly sturdy in build, but gaudy and fanciful in decoration, often featuring lucky wide-open eyes on their prows to help in guiding them over the pathless seas.

Sturdiness was more important than grace in the fishing boats of Bazare, for the surf which rolled in on the beach came straight from the wild, cold global ocean. And the offshore swells were far from gentle.

Though the sea stretched calm and glittering this day, under the hot suns, by next day, it may be smashing rough. This was why the boats were pulled high on the beach, hauled there for safekeeping by teams of oxen who now laid placidly about on the sand.

The boats, like the fishing folk themselves, were said to date back to when the first colonists of seagoing tradesmen had landed. To gaze into the stern, dark faces of the seafaring villagers, hints of the wide tapestry from the known galaxy could be seen.

Unling females were busy at a dozen tasks—sorting fish, spreading some of the pilchards out in the shiny, salty ranks to dry, mending nets piling high their baskets with silvery harvest—these females were more somberly dressed than their check-trouser males. But all over Un, females managed a flourish of bright aprons and bright scarves over drab dresses and wore hoops of gold in their ears. Everywhere they walked with the grace born of balancing burdens on the head, be the burden a basket of fish, a tall clay water jug with an ancestry as old as that of the boats, a bundle of laundry, or a wide, shallow basket of vegetables topped with a bunch of fire-bright flowers.

Fiercest and most independent of Unling females were the 'varinas', the witty, vivacious fish-spouses. When they reached the market place with their baskets, the real fun began, for the Unling loved to bargain, and the great art was in knowing how much to overprice at the start and when, after lively banter, to relent and clinch the deal.

The market, of course, offered more than fish. Other provincial females had risen at dawn or before to bring in their vegetables.

Over the winding, hilly lanes they walked barefoot, with heavily laden broad baskets on their heads, clutching their shawls more snugly against the early morning chill. Out at the highway they waited for the rattle and chug of the Bazare-bound bus to sound around the curve.

Before the bus reached town each day, the roof was packed with baskets, the seats with chattering females. At the stop in town, the baskets were handed down, and the females, hoisting them briskly to their heads, started to jog trot for the market square, for first come often meant first sold.

At the beach, the greater part of the fleet's catch was sold at auction for canning and export. The Unling, who had a genius for doing things a little differently from other people, had their own individual auction technique. Instead of calling for bids, starting low and having bidders top each other until a batch went to the highest bidder, the Unling auctioneer started with a hundred and counted backward with astonishing speed. Thus the first bid was always the highest; the trick, for the buyer, lay in outguessing competitors, getting a bid in ahead of others, yet not extravagantly early.

The pilchards, which were canned in excellent native olive oil, had won a worldwide market for themselves. Indeed, fishing was the planet's second most important industry with tunny, gadus, and shellfish helping to keep the fleets plying the year round.

## CHAPTER TWO:

Far to the north from Bazare, the huge fishing boats, which lay tilted on the sands of the deep bathing beaches, were differently fashioned, with high, jutting prows and sterns sweeping about in a full half-circle curve. And back from the northern coast lay the lagoons where the seaweed gathers plied their trade, for fish was not the only valuable harvest yielded by the sea.

Salt was collected on the open flats, and seaweed, high in mineral content, was gathered on boats called 'moliceiros'. These were slender, far too delicate in line for the rigors of the open sea; they swept up elegantly to a swan-necked prow, with amidships dipping to the water line for ease in raking aboard the water-heavy weeds.

The sailors, wearing short white tunics and helmets, poled their way about the weed beds, raking up the seaweed into piles so high that from the shore it seemed that the boats must surely be sinking under the load. Sometimes the males waded out into the icy waters, with their long-handled rakes; but the fortunate ones had the quaint and lovely boats, each the work of a master craftsman whose skill was the product of many generations.

Not all Unling fishing fleets had the charm of a long and colorful heritage. Many boats were equipped with motors and radio; instead of setting their nets and waiting for the fish to fill them, these could move swiftly to spots where schools of pilchard or tunny had been sighted. The time-hallowed traditions of Un's males of the sea centered around the colorful, highly individualistic craft and their sturdy farers, still often clad in the bright, black and yellow woolen shirts and black stocking caps which had been the garb of their fathers for long generations back. Before setting sail, they still gathered bareheaded on the beaches to receive the blessing of the local magistrate and the prayers of the villagers for a good catch and a safe return from the sea.

Neb Mafan was the foreman of his clan's inland ranch and son to Dajal and V'Quorgroban Mafan. The second of three children, Neb was hotheaded, short-tempered, and very fast with a gun. Always spoiling for a fight and frequently wearing his signature leather gloves, Neb took the slightest offense to the Mafan name personally and quickly made his displeasure known, as often with his fists as with his vociferous shouts.

But this day was a one away from the ranch and the fishing fleets below the main thoroughfare of Bazare. It was also the day of his birth. Surrounded not by his family, but rather two of the males he supervised and directed. All three stood before the town's local libations establishment the *Briny Red: Toast of Bazare Waterfront.*

"So, this is what you males think I want for a present on the day of my birth?" Neb asked. "Huh?"

"Well, like it says, Boss," Izagfor Uhuspin answered with a winsome smile. "It's the toast of the Bazare waterfront."

"Uh-huh."

"It's really something."

"Yeah…" Neb hesitated, turning away from the building issuing pitchy music and even higher-pitched female laughter.

"Drinks are on us!" Sonav Hegno offered.

"I do appreciate this," Neb said. "But I have got to meet my younger brother's transport in less than an hour…"

"Well, then," Sanov urged, "let's get inside, Boss, time's a'wastin…"

"This is really, *really* thoughtful of you two," Neb cut off Hegno in midsentence. "But…" with a pivot he was scooping the other's elbows in his hands and ushering them towards the *Briny Red's* front double door entrance, "…drunks are on me!"

Within seconds all three were inside the saloon and being greeted eagerly by females adorned in low cut, high-hemmed revealing garments. Sonav's and Izagfor's escorts quickly ushered them off to the bar, while Neb's lingered.

"Want to buy me a drink?" she asked, her voice held an innocent huskiness to it. She fluttered her transparent adipose inner eyelids that covered all of her two eyeballs in quick succession.

"I will if you are Briny Red," Neb smiled courteously. "The toast of the Bazare waterfront."

From the upper floor's balcony railing came the pleasant tone of the proprietress herself. "She's not, but why not buy her a drink anyway?" she asked, pleasantly.

A fiery female atypical of all her contemporaries surrounding her. Like all Unlings her morphology was that of a hairless, tailless squamate, yet the shape held firmly in the garment she wore far surpassed any allure of any of the other females in the establishment could have over Neb. His vertical pupils dilated. Entranced, his gazed followed her as she carefully and purposefully descended the stairs to the ground floor.

All eyes were upon her as she moved, glittering sequins embedded in her vermilion dermis seemed to spotlight every muscled action. Like all Unlings, her skin was permeable to water. Gas exchange took place through cutaneous respiration and this allowed adults the option when underwater to respire without rising to the surface of water when swimming.

"Well, now," Neb proclaimed, "you're just like my workers' said, you are far better than a birthing-day gateau."

"Happy Birthing Day, Rancher," Briny Red cooed. Then she turned to the lounge at-large adding, "Females, we're having a birthing-day party!"

"Woo-hoo! A party!" came in unison from the lot of both patrons and staff.

"Which way?" Neb asked.

"This way."

Briny Red gestured for Neb to follow his workers and their escorts into a private back room. As she passed the bar, she instructed the bartender, "Send in a set of *drinks* and see that we are not disturbed. We're having a birthing-day party."

The male responded to her intonation and wink and moved to pull a bottle of brown bracer from the bar-back shelving with one appendage, while with the other several stacked drinking glasses. All were placed on an empty tray on the bar counter's top.

When Neb and Briny Red arrived in the room, the party was already in full swing with the aid of the two female escorts. One was already on a table twisting about in full dance mode to the background music from the lounge. The other had her arms slung over Sonav's neck while singing a traditional birthing-day song, slightly off-key.

The door slid opened and in walked the first female who approached Neb when he had entered the noisy bar area. She proffered glasses filled to their rims with a diluted watery liquid, with a half-smile to the males.

Cheers and a toast to Neb Mafan rang all around the small circle cavorting and singing in his honor. Each of the males downed the liquor without a second thought. It did not take more than a few swings of dancing to have Izagfor Uhuspin collapsing into a drunken stupor on the floor, followed quickly by Sonav Hegno. By the time Neb realized something was terribly, terribly wrong, dark vision was closing in on his peripheral vision and the joyful faces of the four females took on a sinister cosh as oblivion rushed in to claim him too.

In a hauntingly echo, Briny Red's voice coaxed him on into that darkness, saying, "Why fight it? Just *relaxxxx*…" while at the same time she removed his personal portable communicator from his vest pocket.

***

The Mafan Ranch exceeded 1,000 acres and had the Douro River running through it. The main house or 'Mansion' first level had a foyer where the main staircase draped down from a wraparound balcony to a main front room which also acted as sometimes the parlor, to the right a study but also the room where the family played billiards and would talk and play games, to the left of the parlor their gun room.

One could also access the dining room which would take them to the kitchen and if around another door it would bring back out to the parlor. Also, from the kitchen a back or side door to the barn beyond but also a door to the servants' bedrooms.

Upstairs a long hallway, the first door to the right was the master suite and bath, then followed by secondary bedrooms for others in the family, down further to the far-left guest rooms, and bathroom after that. The hallway dead-ended with the door which led up to the finished attic.

A glorious home for such a humble and small fishing village community family not involved in the local trade of seafood marketing, but rather ranching cattle and horses. The estate was set way inland from the coastal Bazare town and its docks. Regardless of its grandeur, its residence were simple reptilianids that basked in family and the celebration of each birth occurring within its clan.

This day was in line with the ancestral-old tradition of birthing cake and iced cream celebrations. The main dining room had been set up buffet-style for the guests awaiting their host-of-honor to arrive. The air was filled with anticipation as well as frustration from the surprise-party's guests.

Dajal and V'Quorgroban Mafan looked at each other nervously at the delayed arrival of their second child, Neb. He was already an hour past due from picking up Narrtrok at the transport station.

"I cannot imagine why they are not here yet," Dajal whispered into her spouse's ear, stifling irritation. She closed her personal portable communicator. "No signal getting through to Neb's com."

"Maybe the transport was late," V'Quorgroban soothed.

The 'whoosh' of the main door to the house followed by the scruff of footsteps on the plush foyer carpeting had Mafan getting everyone's attention in a quiet as possible way. "*Shhhh!* Here they come!" he announced through a forced whisper.

Dajal's face relaxed and lit-up with excitement as she turned to face the opened dining room doorway with the others assembled. "Light the candles," she hushed to a servant by the serving board.

With a nod, the male used a lighter to put a single flame on top of twenty-nine candles decorating the cream-icing birthing-day cake. On its facing, in frosting cursive script spelling out *Happy Birthing-Day, Neb*

Aera Mafan was the eldest daughter to Dajal and V'Quorgroban. She was somewhat self-absorbed, bold and forward. Far from demure, she performed daring stunts and rode astride, like her brothers. So, her gasp was uncharacteristic when she spied only her youngest brother Narrtrok enter through the dining room doorway, traveling case in hand.

"Where's Neb?" she asked, stunned.

"I do not know; he wasn't at the station when my transport came in."

"Why didn't you wait for him?" V'Quorgroban chided. "You were to make sure he got here."

"I did. I waited an hour." Narrtrok placed his case in the capable hands of a servant who exited to take it to the male's upstairs room. "And, no signal from his com. I tried several times to reach him while I waited."

"Maybe somebody bought him a birthday drink, or something," suggested one of the guests.

V'Quorgroban thumbed his forehead. "That's right!" he remembered. "Izagfor and Sonav were going to buy him a drink. He's probably with them."

"Where did they go?" Narrtrok asked.

"They could be any number of places." V'Quorgroban huffed.

Dajal smiled, saying, "Well it's not Neb's fault. After all, he did not know about the party. If anyone, we should blame that … hmmm… that… what's her name? Briny Red?"

The complement of assembled friends and associates chuckled in amusement. The reputation of the establishment was well known throughout the Bazare community.

"Nothing gets by you, does it?" V'Quorgroban laughed openly.

Dajal followed and soon the entire room was aloud with gaiety.

"Who is she?" Aera asked innocently.

"Polite ladies would not even mention her name," V'Quorgroban feigned nonchalantly.

"I'll try and restrain myself," Dajal guffawed. "In the future. I do hope that Neb can tear himself away soon."

V'Quorgroban gathered himself, then announced, "I think I'll go into town and find him. Bring him back home for a piece of gateau."

With an affectionate kiss to his spouse on her nearest cheek, Mafan was away. His sudden absence left a void within the party's frivolous atmosphere. The sudden departure seemed to suck the very air from the room. Dajal looked about unsettled.

Narrtrok broke the odd mood by filling a stemmed glass with champagne and raising it into the air, toasting, "Happy Birthing-day, Neb, wherever you are!"

## CHAPTER THREE:

The rocky highlands of Un were composed of wild, desolate scenery. Lonely and isolated air. The cattle in the rocky hillside pastures, the horses and burros on the dusty mountain roads, even the people were small of size, as if they had been shut away too long from any contact with the big world beyond.

The topography a natural fortress, yet it never had been able to defend itself, due principally to lack of population. In precolonial times, the highland inhabitants learned to fear the scrape of enemy keels on their beaches, the bonfires of invaders blazing in the night. So they built themselves a network of watch-tower-fortresses which still stood into modern times.

The round stone towers, about thirty feet across at the base and diminishing in size as they rose, were called 'nuraghis' and their ruins dotted the landscape everywhere. They loomed up on rocky mountain peaks; they surmounted ridges; they commanded views down dramatic gorges and river valleys. The large ones were apparently equipped to withstand siege, often with a well or spring within the walls, with niches at the entrance in which sentries could hide, with stairways leading to platforms or second floor above. Between these large towers stood smaller ones so spaced that signals could be passed along from one tower to the next down the chain.

Winds had sculpted the rocks, and the topsoil between them was so thin that only by patient and careful scratching with sticks could it be tilled here and there for a crop. Much of the topsoil was lost with the forests, ravished by speculators who slashed the trees with savage thoroughness, burning the wood for charcoal to sell. Now there were only scattered groves of cork trees, some glowing red where the bark had been newly stripped; the pale gray-green of olive groves as stooped and weathered as the rocks themselves; some orange, prickly pears, chestnuts, oaks, and pines—and mile after mile of bare and dusty upland rock.

A scant crop of barley growing among these rocks was reaped as gently as the picking of flowers. For each precious grain had to be preserved if the farmers were to have a crop worth of the name. A more unusual mountain harvest came as chestnuts. A simple shaking of the chestnut tree was all it took for stout limbs to one by one send the nut burs tumbling to the ground.

Boys and girls scampered, armed with tongs or pairs of sticks, picking up the prickly nuts by the apron or basketful. The outer shells were broken with stones or other hard objects and the nuts were stored away to serve as a vegetable throughout the lean and chilly winter.

As for the barley, it was taken to the mill for grinding into flour. The mill was a simple one, often in a home; and in its structure and the set of the stones it was usually quite like those known from the ruins of ancient civilizations, were in use two thousand years ago.

Deep within the foundry's bowels, Briny Red led two of her hired male henchmen to drag the limp bodies of Neb Mafan, Izagfor Uhuspin, and Sonav Hegno inside and be deposited unglamorously on a dusty floor. Seeing that they were secure, Briny Red and her complement made a quick exit, locking the basement door behind them. She did have another business to run.

***

V'Quorgroban Mafan was educated, refined, and the calmer of the Mafan clan who handled all the family's legal and business affairs. While a skilled businessman, he preferred the law to settle disputes, but he was known to resort to frontier justice and violence when necessary. His gentle nature was being tested as he waited not-so-patient within the *Briny Red* lounge to see its proprietress for some answers to the whereabouts of his middle son. His absence in the establishment and the lack of answers to questions about his presence in the saloon not meeting his expectations had his parental intuition tingling.

Every person since the day they were born had been cataloged, numbered, and voice imprinted. Everyone, even enemies, had records of each other. To not to be able to locate someone in the modern era was an anomaly.

Something very wrong had happened here not too long ago, he sensed. Mafan would have to handle this situation very delicately moving forward.

He approached a like-able barmaid by the counter and asked, "Kind of quiet in here, isn't it?" He gestured toward the sparse patronage within the tables and chairs area. "I have heard this place was an exciting place."

"Well," she cooed. "It's still early." Moving a delicate arm to a bottle on the bar top, she asked, "What will it be?"

"I have been trying to talk to your boss," he said. "Is she around?"

"Maybe."

Ironically, the back door slid aside and in strolled a curvy Briny Red. Mafan's gaze was too intense not to meet it. Her attempts to divert her eyes were unsuccessful as the stoic male approached her from the bar area. Each was familiar to the other.

"Hello, Caelia," he greeted with a nod of his head.

"Mister Mafan," came a respective reply. Looking over his shoulder at the barmaid, she called out, "Rebexa, give him whatever he wants."

The seductive youth sauntered over to stand beside Mafan expectantly.

"Make sure the glass is clean," Briny 'Caelia' Red insisted. "Mister Mafan doesn't like to get his fingers dirty."

Mafan took the jab in good humor and to the youthful female to his side, said, "I'll have little Armagnac." Turning to look directly at the female across from him, he said meaningfully, "If you will join me."

Moving to the nearest table, Caelia said, "We have three drinks here: beer, whisky, and gin."

Pulling out a chair for the proprietress, Mafan answered, "Then I'll have whiskey."

Over her shoulder, Caelia instructed to the waiting barmaid, "One whiskey."

Rebexa made her way back to the bar to fulfill the request. As one, the two took their respective seats. Each seemingly knowing more about the other than what either one was willing to reveal verbally. An odd silence settled between them; but the silence shared by friends—yet perhaps old friends.

"Do you always make it a practice to check up on old clients?" Caelia smirked.

"Now, Caelia," Mafan replied winsomely. "Remember, we are friends."

"It's a little late for that, isn't it? On account of you, I spent a hundred and eighty days in the House of Corrections. Isn't that what *they* call it?"

Mafan paused as he noticed the swirl of a lacy skirt approach. Rebexa held a tray with a single glass filled with a rich amber liquid. He waited for her to deposit the drink and depart before he answered, "Now there wasn't very much I could do about that. Was there?"

"Wasn't there?" Caelia countered. "The judge was an old friend of your family. You could have fixed it up with him."

"That is not the way justice is served," Mafan replied with a small salute of his proffered glass. He gently sipped and waited for Caelia's response.

Leaning forward, Briny Red locked eyes with the older male, asking, "What do you want?"

Mafan nodded. "All right. I just want you to know that I am sincerely sorry about the House of Corrections. I wish I could have helped you."

"Do you really think you could have intervened?"

"If you were innocent."

"What difference does it make?" Caelia leaned back into her chair. "You went your way, I went mine." She smiled warmly. "What brings a fancy businessman like you to an establishment like this?"

"You want me to be honest?" Mafan leaned forward on his elbows, crossing his forearms while looking Caelia directly in her eyes. After she nodded, he went on, "You. I have thought about you a great deal since you walked out of my office that day. There were a lot of things we did not get to say. I wish we could have just gotten to know each other better as …well … male and female instead of client and supplier. And, when I heard you had started a business of your own here in Bazare…well… here I am."

"Get to know one another?" Caelia grinned. "How would we do that, Mister Mafan?"

"First by calling me V'Quorgroban or 'Roban for short," he smiled. "And, secondly by having lunch with me."

"And, then?"

"Well, I would not be much of a businessman if I told you all my tragedy, now would I?"

Caelia chuckled out loud and nodded. "All right, 'Roban, I'll have lunch with you."

"Good!" Mafan sat up straight and broadened his smile.

"But," Caelia interjected. "On two conditions."

"Name them."

"We do not talk about my case. That is over."

"Agreed. You served your sentence." Mafan picked up his half-emptied glass, adding, "And, I am sure you would not go back into the trafficking business. Would you?"

The ginger-skinned female seemed to blush, her shapely jaw dropped as if in shock at such a notion. "I never admitted I was in the trafficking business to begin with," she reminded him. "Remember?"

Mafan nodded. "I remember. Now, what's it the second condition?"

"I want to pick the place."

"Anywhere you say."

Caelia cocked her left eyebrow, answering, "Well, how about … the Mafan Ranch?" She could see the comfortability over the thought waning. "You can tell your spouse I would like a formal invitation in writing." With that statement, she rose confidently. There seemed to be a power-shift at the table between the two; she held the upper hand. "That is how it is done in your part of town, isn't it?"

Mafan rose to meet her stance. "Sometimes."

Briny Red simply smiled and bowed her head, "Good day, 'Roban."

As the female returned to her duties of managing the saloon, Mafan felt a sudden stirring in the pit of his stomach, as if a trapdoor had been suddenly sprung.

## CHAPTER FOUR:

While the females of the inlands of Bazare busied themselves with the spindle, loom, and needle, their male counterparts occupied themselves with watching their flocks, some of them were tending crops, some stripping cork trees of bark or hacking blocks of limestone from the area's quarries, or weaving sturdy baskets out of reeds. All the while others drew their livelihood from the waters around it. Each villager had a different specialty.

Mafan took noticed of his townsmen as he drove his single passenger coupe transport back to the Mansion. His mind filled with 'what ifs' and 'revenge scenarios'. Directing the small vehicle through the Ranch's primary gate toward the statuesque silhouette of the main house, he took notice of the three suns slipping into dusk before him. Night was leading him home.

The main level of the house was quiet when Mafan entered through the front door. It seemed as if everyone had retired to their respective quarters. Taking the sweeping staircase up to the second floor only got him halfway, his younger son's voice called to him from the downstairs parlor.

Aera was there too. Both children held concern in their gazes as they watched their father enter the room fully.

"Neb?" asked Narrtrok.

Mafan shook his head sadly. "No sign of him anywhere in town."

All three exchanged looks of concern. They remained quiet as each took a moment to digest what that statement could mean.

"Son," Mafan said. "It is just a suspicion, but I … I think your brother has been trafficked."

"Trafficked!" Aera shouted.

Mafan hushed her, concerned the exclamation would rouse Dajal. "Is your mother asleep?" he asked the two.

"She's reading in bed," Narrtrok said.

Mafan took a moment to collect his thoughts before presenting his hypothesis. "Briny Red was a client of mine before I met your mother. She was known to work for a notorious crimp named Daviad Ayden."

"Crimp?" asked Aera.

"Yes," Mafan explained, "someone engaged in this form of kidnapping is known as a crimp. They deliver live bodies to ships that need crews."

"You think Neb and his males are already on a ship?"

"I don't know, Aera. All I do know is that Neb and Izagfor and Sonav are nowhere to be found in town, and they are not here. And, Briny Red once spent over six months in corrections for enticing males and females to sea and out into Space against their wills. There is a good chance she is still in the same business."

"But, Bazare is just a river port," Aera said.

"That does not make any difference," Mafan explained. "They could be short of crew, and when that happens they'll take whatever they can get."

Narrtrok lowered his eyes in realization, adding, "And never return with the same crew."

Aera gasped, "What do you mean?""

The voice that answered her was not the deep baritone or bass of her brother or father, but yet the bell-like pitch of her mother. "It means," Dajal said from the parlor entrance, "we may never see Neb or the others again."

All three males went instantly quiet. They watched the regal female step completely into the living space. Her eyes wise with unwanted knowledge. She looked at her daughter with purpose, continuing to say, "There are only two ways of escape from those ships. Desertion. Which makes it almost impossible to get back … or … death at sea or in vacuum." She squared her shoulders and jaw and met her spouse's eyes firmly. "Am I exaggerating 'Roban?"

Mafan slowly shook his head remorsefully. "No," he seemed to moan.

"Then why are we just standing here?!" Aera declared. "Let's go get the constable!"

"No, no, Aera," Mafan snapped out of his doldrums. "I've seen this thing before in the highlands. If the constable goes to Briny Red and asks questions, then she and her cohorts will get rid of the evidence."

Aera shook her head confused. "I don't understand."

"Neb and Izagfor and Sonav," Mafan replied meaningfully. "They are the only evidence against them."

"Well if the law cannot help…"

Mafan cut his daughter's declaration off and interjected, "If Neb and the others are not back by morning, we'll just have to help ourselves." Turning to his remaining son, he said, "Narrtrok, you know the Mariner's Paradise Auberge? It's on the waterfront."

The youth nodded. "I know of the place."

"Well, they do not know you. So I want you to check in there in the morning and find out anything you can. Aera, you go to the harbormaster's office and get me a complete list of all incoming and outgoing ships. It'll be my job to find out what I can from Briny Red." He looked from his children to his mate, adding, "I've invited her here for lunch tomorrow." Dajal stiffened and he explained, "She'll come. But, only if she gets a written invitation from you."

It took a few moments for Dajal to digest the request. Her mind swimming with doubts and developments of events. Exhaling she asked, "'Roban, do we have enough time?"

"I'm not sure we have any time at all."

The truth hung in the air and in their collective thoughts as dusk darkened through the sectional bay windows into the ebon cosh of evening, tripping the auto-sensory lights to heighten the lumen count of the parlor. It was if a ghost had walked amongst them.

\*\*\*

Into everyone's life some sorrow came, and the folk of Un had learned to accept their share of grief and care along with their daily work and joys. When death came, as it must, the relatives followed heavy-hearted at a respectful distance as the loved one was brought to the kirche. Before entering the presence of the dead, each donned the cowl of mourning—a dark shawl—and the endless chants and rhyming laments were led by professional mourners whose classic ritual went back to ancient times. Thus the Unlings paid their respects to death as a part of the natural cycle of life, as normal as birth or breathing.

From Neb Mafan's perspective he was not sure which scenario he had found himself in: the dead or the mourner. He was lying flat on his back against a very hard and uncomfortable surface. Dark swirled his vision in a semi-conscious fog as he decided whether or not to become fully aware of his surroundings or slip peacefully back into oblivion.

He heard groaning off to either side of him in his disorientation, causing his head to instantly ache. As if a sledgehammer had suddenly been used as his waking bell. He too groan in discomfort. The 'hangover' was the worse he had ever experienced as his special senses were roused one by one, after sound came smell. Flour. Dust. Mold.

Each new scent more unpleasant that it's prior. He touched his unmarred face expectantly, then his head—all was well--and he shifted to his side in a fetal position before pushing himself upright into a seated position, at least he thought he was sitting instead of lying. Then came sight. His eyes burned and a piercing light stabbed at his occipital interpretation centers. White blindness overwhelmed him and he gasped audibly.

Blinking helped clear his vision. He was facing a horizontal planked wall. He held out his hands till they touched its solidity and then used the spaces between the wooden slats to climb into a standing position. His knees protested. Gaining some equilibrium he steadied his stance.

Where was he?! His mind screamed. *What had happened?!*

In his peripheral vision he saw a slumped Izagfor and then Sonav in opposite corners of the room they all were occupying. He approached the nearest, Izagfor. Shaking him, he tried to awaken the moaning male. "Hey! Hey!" Neb coaxed. The worker awoke suddenly, startled. "Are you all right?"

Weakly, Izagfor nodded. "What happened? Where are we?"

Neb shrugged and took notice that Sonav was slowly coming around and had shifted from his back to all-fours into a lunge with his right leg and attempting to push himself up to stand. Seeing that his companions were none the worse than himself, he began to examine their location.

Four wooden walls, a slatted floor, a high ceiling covered in dustwebs, a barred window that looked out onto a panoramic highland view with a mighty river coursing south through its rocky landscape beyond. The rushing of the rapids could be heard clearly now that their collective murkiness had begun to dissipate.

"We're near the highland's river system," Izagfor identified.

Neb nodded and felt his dry throat crackle as he guffawed, "Some birthing day party!"

The sounds of footfalls made all three notice a closed door on the opposite wall. As the footmarks drew closer to the sealed portal, Neb and the two other males snapped sober and jumped into action by taking point around the threshold. It opened abruptly, affording a squadron of males to storm in. In the front was a collection of disheveled males looking as lost as the three felt, behind were mariners pushing at the rear.

Neb waited till the disorderly lot passed by him before planting a double-fist meaningfully against the nap of the first mariner's neck. The male fell like a dropped stone. Sonav and Izagfor teamed up on two other mariners while a third grabbed Neb by the scruff of his shirt and set about to club him with his raised truncheon.

"Belay that action!" came a brass-toned male voice from behind everyone. "You want to damage the goods?!"

The tableau froze. All looked to the source of the proclamation. In strolled a dapper male suited in a contemporary suit, consisting of knee-length breeches worn over stockings, tailcoat cut high over the top of the breeches, collar turned up and a ruffled cravat worn at the neck. A bowler hat topped the dandy's bald cranium in true steam punk fashion.

Seeing that he had gathered all concerned attentions, the prissy male smiled and added, "This way!"

With that, he jabbed his right fist fully into Neb's abdomen, causing the male to lurch over in agony. As he recovered, a fierce slap across the face sent him to the floor unconscious. Adjusting his askew suit jacket, the newcomer regained his prim demeanor unruffled.

***

There were three habitable zones to most life-giving worlds: the air, the land, and lastly, the sea. And those who had claimed either of the first two had clearly not been designed to get their feet wet.

The sun of Un, slightly redder than its sister stars, glinted sharply off mirror-like swells, struck the small silvery splinters excitedly and raced on to illumine the shores of Bazare. The incredible lushness of the sea was mesmerizing to those who plowed beneath its surface as was the overabundance of life that comprised such lushness. To most, it was the constant motion that contrasted so heavily with the stilted, jointed world of air-breathers.

Everything submarine was part of a single, unending underwater ballet—a dancing ecology, where every inhabitant from the lowliest worm or plant to the bemuscled and fanged carnivore knew its assigned steps and performed uncomplainingly a perpetual choreography.

This was the world of green glass through which the Mer of Un probed their leisurely paths. Whether ascending or descending gradually, they eventually leveled off about a dozen meters from a sandy bottom.

For gather-hunter Arhun, a resident mermale, he was swimming outward from his crèche. His unique anatomy allowed his lower extremities the ability to adapt from deep watery pressures, to shallower terrestrial places. The skeletal structure of his legs could give the appearance of being almost boneless, with the feet metamorphosing into true flippers, supple and flexible. Yet, when needed the reorganizing bones would quickly transform to allow his kind to walk on land.

Clusters of amber moss sequined with phosphorescent shells and tiny crawlers drifted lazily in the gentle current. Tight formations of brilliantly hued fish of various sizes and shapes wheeled and spun in disturbed silicate cloudlets, larger solitary swimmers observed enviously.

The bipedal finned mermale moved in a widening spiral, now well out from his place of origin. Finally, on the fourth curve out, Arhun encountered the continental shelf. It was the area of seabed around a large landmass where the sea was relatively shallow compared with the open ocean.

The continental shelf was geologically part of the Un continental crust. Here was a good place for hunting and gathering. Unlike the cultivated seabed of his home, gardens laid out in an unearthly but undeniably artificial fashion, this was pure wilderness, the wild.

Arhun found it odd that the shelf seemed deserted. Everything was in hiding. At first it was a curiosity to discover why, but as he continued to swim closer and closer along the angled incline into swallower and swallower waters, the reason became self-evident. Air-breathers. In his haste to solve the mystery, he had inadvertently wandered into an air-breather population center's harbor. He had to admit that he partly had come here on purpose. He was a curious creature and had visited this forbidden territory before. Many befores.

Acute hearing alerted Arhun to the vibrations of air-sourced sounds, voices. Ripples of conversation reverberated like sonar throughout the waterways, forcing old instincts in the marine life to shy away from the area and seek safer, quieter waters.

Being sentient, Arhun could not help himself as his curiosity overcame racial fear. Mer young had saved their kind once, but it was not a happy outcome.

The words coming through the water were muffled and incoherent. Being an experienced gather-hunter, Arhun had taught himself parts of the air-breather or Caecilian language, but always from a safe distance—slightly submerged alongside the hull of an anchored ship, under the pylons of a pier. But, never had he dared to merge so close to docks and moored sailing vessels. Never in the light of day.

The dock in Bazare was the area of water next to a group of artificially-made structures that were involved in the handling of boats and ships (usually on or near the shore) or such structures themselves. The enclosed area of water was used for loading, unloading, building or repairing ships. Bazare's dock had been created by building enclosing harbor walls into an existing natural water space. All this Arhun knew.

The air-breather community was built along a hillside into a valley. Stone columns stood beside the waterway, topped with pedestals upon which stood strange statues.

There were other structures across the valley, some of them similar to the ones he'd seen before in other coastal gathering places. There were more patterns and symbols painted on these buildings, differing in color and shape. It lent them an alien, ethereal beauty.

Swimming deeper into the harbor along the pylons of the docks, the structures were quite different here from the larger stone buildings he'd seen further up from the coast on the hillside and included many built on stilts. Incorporated into the village, grounded on the curved beach's bank, was the harbor proper. Moored cargo ships of various sizes competed for space and attention with the smaller fishing boats hauled out of the surf and grounded on the beach itself.

Rising just enough so his smooth aquamarine scalp and brow-line rose above the waterline, Arhun first sought to observe the source of the air-breather voices. Like a binocular periscope his eyes scanned the surface and then above.

Two male air-breathers were standing close to the end of the wharf. Dressed in traditional garments that covered their entire physique—*how unnatural*!—they had a nonchalant manner between them. Allowing his shell-like bilateral ears to also emerge, Arhun clearly heard the conversation the two were involved in.

"Gotta light, Stranger?" asked 'Roban Mafan of the other male who had approached him from the wharf's lodging building.

Dressed in traditional sailor ware, Narrtrok sauntered over to his father and removed a portable metallic lighting device from his pea coat jacket's right pocket. The handheld device ignited at the touch of a contact point. Placing the small flame against an extended fumarole ignited its tip enough to allow it to smolder.

Mafan nodded grateful at the disguised Narrtrok. In a low tone he asked, "Anything?"

"Not yet." Narrtrok disengaged the lighter and returned it to the jacket pocket.

The elder nodded again and said loud enough for anyone within earshot to hear, "Much appreciated." Then he walked away, leaving his son alone on the wharf's edge.

Arhun was suddenly struck at the handsomeness of the air-breather. The strong line of his jaw bespoke of a great warrior, the broadness of his chest and shoulders of a fierce hunter, the trim tapering of his waist into his loins of great virility, the thickness of his thighs and legs of someone who was not idle.

All great physical qualities in a sentient being. This male was no parasite.

Compared to the elfin lithe and small-frame of Arhun, this air-breather was a giant; a quarter more than his height and weight. That alone took the merman's gill-breath away. Luckily at some point up the evolutionary line, the two shared a common amphibian ancestral branch. A sarcopterygian fish with lungs and bony-limbed fins, features that were helpful in adapting to dry land or existing in deep water.

Of all the animals, fish being sexually the most fluid.

Uniquely, the Sarcopterygii changed routinely from female to male. Others did the opposite, from male to female. Still others could switch back and forth depending on the circumstance, such as a variety of coral-dwelling gobies. And at least one species, the mangrove killifish, lived a fully hermaphroditic existence, self-fertilizing for their entire reproductive lives.

For the Mer, they were 'sequential hermaphrodites' known as 'protogynous': switching from female to male. In most Mer, some started out lives as male (Hunters), some changed from female to male at some point (Gather-Hunters), and some remained as females (Gathers) for the full duration of their lives.

The 'size advantage' was at the root for the change. It was advantageous to be of a different gender once it had reached a certain size. In Mer society, since one dominant male held sway over a harem of smaller females, it was handy to become male in later life when larger. The gender of most marine inhabitants was not determined by chromosomes: birds and mammals in fact were unusual in having the gender of offspring almost universally determined in this way.

Amphibians, reptiles, and fish employed a variety of methods to determine the gender of their offspring. Frequently, temperature determined gender – most fish preferentially developed as male in warmer water.

Mer gonads contained the precursor cells for both ovarian and testicular tissue, a rapid flood of either estrogen or testosterone-like hormones flipped a switch and caused new tissue to develop.

It took months for an individual Mer female to turn into a male.

Even though the Mer lived in water, 'junk genes' still afforded them bipedalism and functional 'lungs' for temporary bouts out of water when hunting necessitated leaving the sea to find food in times of famine. If anything, the Mer and the air-breathers were kissing cousins, separated in only how air was acquired and processed in their respective bodies. Both resembling a bald snub-nosed langur variant.

Arhun rarely found air-breathers interesting. Mere fish-eaters, killers of all that was tranquil below the waves. But, every now and then an exception occurred. This day had presented such.

There was something peaceful and vulnerable in the air-breather's countenance and demeanor. One that was akin to the Mer. This air-breather was no despoiler of the vital links in the cycle of life.

His wished, just this once, he had the courage to break the Mer prime directive of non-contact with surface dwellers. To know this air-breather as a brethren and perhaps … more. It seemed that this surface dweller knew he was being watched, for he did not move from his spot on the planked pier. He stayed and allowed his sparkling eyes to stare out onto the horizon, as if to spy something specific out 'there'.

Arhun almost gasped aloud when he heard the Caecilian matter-of-factly say toward the waterline, yet keeping his eyes on the horizon, "I see you there. Watching me."

For several moments, Arhun froze. He dared not reveal himself if the air-breather was talking to someone out of sight on the dock. Yet, no one else appeared. He'd become adept at reading expressions, realizing that the eyes and face told so much about a person's intentions long before their actions revealed themselves. That had saved his life more than once.

This air-breathing male was inscrutable. He looked capable and calm, but his eyes and face gave nothing away. He might as well have been wearing a mask.

"I need your help. You've been passively observing the goings-on here at the docks and in the harbor. You might have vital information that I need to save the life of my brother. Meet me at the reeds at the delta's edge if you wish to speak to me in person," the attractive Caecilian said, moving away from the slip's edge. "Please and thank you!"

Excited, curious, and with interpretation, Arhun eased himself away from the surface and underwater. He swam swiftly away from the harbor, round to the undeveloped part of the port to where the fresh water from deep inland mountains spread out like a muddy fan with the sea. There, he waited in silence to see if he had heard the air-breather correctly.

The area was a landform created by the deposition of sediment carried by the Douro River as the flow exited its mouth and the entered slower-moving water headed for the sea. A wetland area filled with a bouquet of fern trees, flowering mosses, and reeds. A primordial zone yet untouched by urban development.

"How this place is not packed with people right now," came the Caecilian's voice as his silhouette revealed itself from the wetland shadows startled the Mermale. "Hmmm. I have my ways, trust me, we won't be disturbed. You can come out of the water now."

Tentatively, Arhun slowly rose from the pool and allowed the air to fill his awakened lungs.

Automatically his gill slits sealed as he coughed up pneumatic fluid, taking a deep airy breath in.

Walking fully on to the land, he was in full view of the air-breather. His heart was racing with excitement and trepidation. Being in his natural form, there were no garments to hide within. He stood vulnerable and fully exposed before the air-breather.

They stood in silence, facing and looking at each other in a marshy glade encircled by tall, lushly leaved trees. Small streams wound merrily down the low slope around them.

"You're amazing," the Caecilian praised. His eyes looking the other male up and down like a searchlight. He walked right up to the mermale, smiling broadly. "I may never leave this place. This is my favorite place on the whole of this planet." He paused, enjoying the view. Then realized he had no idea who this other male was, nor vice versa. "Oh, I am so sorry. How rude. I am Narrtrok Mafan. Do you understand me?"

Arhun swallowed hard, trying to find his voice. Using air instead of water as a medium for vocalization took a few times to perfect. But he smiled timidly up at the taller air-breather and replied, "Y-yes… I do… under … understand. I am called Arhun."

"Thank you for meeting me, Arhun," Narrtrok grinned. "I've noticed you around the harbor before. But this day when I saw you watching me… I just had to try and meet you."

"I am flattered," Arhun smiled. "Contact between the Caecilian world and the Mer world is strictly forbidden."

"I know that, everyone knows that," Narrtrok's grin broadened. "So, am I the spineless, savage harpooning fish-eater that is incapable of any feeling you expected? I hope you take the chance to get to know me. Caecilians are individuals. Just because one is an ass, doesn't mean we all are."

Arhun laughed out loud, amused by the other's self-deprecation. "What is this information you seek of me to save your brother?" he asked curious.

"He has been abducted to forcibly crew a ship. I am not sure who took him nor what ship he is being forced to crew."

"I can find that information out for you, if you'd like."

"I'd like that very much," Narrtrok smiled. "I'd be extremely grateful."

There was an uncomfortable pause between as to where the conversation should go next. Arhun was the first to speak.

"This is your favorite place?"

"Yes. And where is yours?"

"Deep within the benthic currents, west of here. The waters there change color," Arhun explained. "As if the currents have moods. The hours, days I have spent chasing the perfect slipstream, so addictive."

Narrtrok stepped closer. "Addicted to the ocean," he chuckled. "Hmmm."

Arhun seemed to laugh at the irony. He looked about the environs and said, "You are right. This place is special."

"And, now with you here," Narrtrok flirted. "It's perfect."

There was a definite, mutual attraction between the two males. Between a Mer and a Caecilia. An air-breather and a water-breather. Stranger pairings had happened before, just not between such different worlds on Un. As if they were two alien species of the same progenitor meeting for the very first time.

"Beyond all reason," Narrtrok said. "I have become infatuated with you. I want to … would you want to …?"

"Yes, I'd like that. To know you more." Arhun turned back toward the water. "Come with me. Into the water."

Slowly the mermale descended under the waterline, slowly looking back at Narrtrok to make sure he was being followed. He held out a beckoning hand.

Narrtrok blushed, "Oh… sure…yep…"

Quickly he disrobed until only his natal skin showed. He smirked as he saw the appreciative expression reflected in Arhun's attractive, aquatic face. He took the proffered palm and allowed himself to be led waist deep into the marsh. The chilled water was refreshing against his hot torso, cooling his loins if only temporarily.

"You are the most incredible being I have ever met," Narrtrok gushed as he was led in a circle by Arhun. "Finally, being able to be near you is thrilling. Wherever you go, I want you to take me with you."

With a laugh of delight, Arhun embraced the air-breather and pushed against the bigger body until it willingly submerged into the opaque subaqueous world. Their inhibitions abandoned in a fluidic dance resembling the ancient mythical Picesian symbol.

## CHAPTER FIVE:

The bar lounge of the *Briny Red* found by V'Quorgroban Mafan were a sparse gathering of male patrons and a lone barkeeper mulling about in typical saloon activities. Taking a pause in his inspection at the bar, he enjoyed a few inhalation and exhalation of his freshly lit fumarole. The smoky nicotine eased the pit of his nervous stomach. There was still the vileness of violation in the air.

A door panel marked PRIVATE slid aside and Caelia 'Briny Red' Saeva emerged from its threshold, electronic tablet in hand. She headed directly to the barkeep oblivious of others in the room.

"Did you really check that shipment of libation barrels?" she asked, obviously miffed. "They are charging us…" She stopped at recognizing the stare of Mafan from across the bar top. "We'll check it later," she changed the line of conversation, handing the tablet to the barkeep and gesturing him away.

In true gentle fashion, Mafa approached Caelia and proffered a small bouquet of blue-violets he had concealed from under his overcoat. "Best of Morning," he greeted.

"Best of Morning," Caelia echoed back, awestruck.

Mafan indicated with an index digit to the small fold of papyrus bended neatly between the blooms of the nosegay. "I hope you enjoy chilled crustacean with a very dry blanch wine," he said.

Caelia opened the folded over piece of paper and read it aloud, "The pleasure of your company at a luncheon this day. Signed, Dajal Mafan."

"And if the cook is in very good form," Mafan humored. "A chestnut soufflot for dessert."

She looked at him with a serious expression. "You're not joking, are you?!"

"V'Quorgroban Mafan rarely jokes."

"Come on now," Caelia snickered. "You think I am a crimp!"

"I never called you a crimp."

"I said 'think'," she corrected. "And that is what you think. Isn't it? That's what you thought when you would not testify on my behalf in my criminal case."

"Caelia, I did not testify on your behalf because you wanted me to bribe a judge."

She huffed and moved away from the bar. "I said I didn't want to talk about that. Look, I run a waterfront bar. That's not against the law, is it?"

"Absolutely not." He moved to stand behind her. "I'll pick you up a sun's zenith."

"No. I do not what to be picked up. I hate that expression," she frowned. "I'll come out to the Ranch alone."

"Alone?"

She turned to face Mafan, holding up the invitation. "I've got my passport, haven't I?"

He simply nodded and made a quiet exit.

\*\*\*

Narrtrok and Arhun's frolicking had taken them away from the inlet marshland and into a cave mouth. Although nervous, Narrtrok was excited.

For the first time in this experience, the unexpected inspired curiosity over fear. The soft slush of the delta rivulets echoed into a greater roar; light quickly faded away. There was not total darkness in the grotto as creatures scurried across the vaulted ceilings, beaming with a bright phosphorescent glow that gave a soft background illumination, like ever-moving stars.

The water was flat and even, the walls steep, and Narrtrok had the distinct impression that some of it had been carved rather than eroded. Suddenly he was in an unknown, mysterious place on his own home planet.

As the two stayed entwined and continued to swim further, their surroundings grew lighter, and eventually they emerged from beneath the hillside of Bazare into another valley. This one was steeper-sided and more enclosed than the wide coastal inlet they had just left. The waterway here was narrower and faster moving, and they quickly drew close to the nearest bank.

The feeder river eventually widened into a lagoon. Incorporated into its banks was a grounded wrecked spacer ship. Its superstructure seemed to be part of the sandy ribbon of water-worn silicate embankment. Its rusted alloyed hull was covered in creeper vines, forming a decoration of angular lines that was colorful.

The vessel was so out of place, Narrtrok blinked a couple of times, shaking his head to clear his vision. Drawing closer to the shoreline, he could just make out its name: *Maiden 1*.

It was as if it had been there always, growing from the rock of the land instead of crashing centuries before, crew already long gone and dead with their descendants unaware of its existence, a place of tragedy and death perhaps for those that had not survived the impact.

Narrtrok had a different interpretation. The grounded spacecraft was almost beautiful, and even where the morning light probed through holes created by rot and time, it looked like it was meant to be.

"It is from the first people to land here on Un," Arhun told him. He led his new paramour out of the water, along the shore toward the ship, through waist-high grasses, and into the grounded spaceship.

It looked larger the nearer they got to it. Narrtrok could see several rusted holes in its hull, and he wondered whether they had been torn there during the ship's final moments or had decayed over time since the wreck. He saw so much here that must have been exclusive to the valley.

Plant life, insects, and several unusual species of small mammal, and unique fowl that danced and sang from the tree canopy. The trees themselves were huge and primeval, towering so high up that their fronds were lost in a haze of mist, thrown up by the steaming temperatures and high humidity. A closed ecosystem, which was truly a wild undiscovered land.

It was also unpredictable. One moment they were pushing through huge ferns, the next they emerged into a wide clearing of knee-high grasses and sparse, thin shrubs. Narrtrok followed Arhun cautious and quiet. Birdsong continued around them.

Crickets sawed away in the high grasses. Arachnids scampered across fern leaves above their heads, shadowy silhouettes running and pausing, running and pausing.

Narrtrok was alert for noise and movement around them.

Arhun led the way in through one of the openings, up a small slope of wreckage, and into an interior passageway. It was cool inside, as if heat from outside could not find its way in.

Lit from several large openings above, the functional corridor had been carved and taken over by the surrounding foliage over the years so that it barely resembled a ship's interior at all. A strange glow emanated from the rents in the hull, speckling the bulkheads with luminescence and catching dust drifting in the air.

"Magnificent," Narrtrok breathed.

Turning a rounded curve in the corridor, Arhun led Narrtrok into an expanded space within the bowels of the downed spacer. Perhaps it had been once been one of the ship's holds, or a high-ceilinged recreation room, but everything about it had changed.

Walls were contoured with dried mud and inundated with creeper vegetation making obscure shapes and images that resembled a bas-relief. Like the deck of the corridors, the floor was made from trodden-down mud, hardened over time into a smooth, concrete-like surface.

High up, the ceiling was open to the sky, but crisscrossed with heavy vines and hanging epiphyte plants, making for an artificial forest canopy. The whole space emitted a strange phosphorescent glow that permeated the entire room.

They were not alone. Small lizards scampered across the bulkheads and floor, skittering out of sight, ducking into crevasses. Spears of sunlight illuminated the large area, cast down through holes rusted into the ceiling and walls.

The place took on a spiritual mien and had depths Narrtrok suspected contained more than simply shadows. Moss grew on rocks, glimmering in the fresh day's light.

Arhun willingly laid back against the warm lichen as the primary climbed quickly to its zenith in the sky. He helplessly gazed up into the inviting eyes of Narrtrok as he mounted onto him. The larger frame not pressing as heavily down on him as he had anticipated. In fact, the touch of Caecilian skin against his Mer dermis was pure pleasure. They kissed deeply just as Narrtrok pushed gently between Arhun's elevated legs into his eager pelvis with his own. Arhun welcomed him into himself with wanton uninhibitedness, they were joined. They shared a mutual aura of desire. The two separated worlds of Un had become one.

Narrtrok explored the mermale's body with his lips, leaving the face, to the neck, onto the chest and below. Arhun had never known such pleasure, fantasized desires now suddenly realized. What natural selection had separated eons past, now joined again in a rhythmic undulation of thrusts and moans of passion unleashed. They were born again.

## CHAPTER SIX:

Aera rendezvous with her father and brother as planned just before sun's zenith at the Mafan Company's corporate office located downtown Bazare. There she would present what she had been sent to retrieve.

"Anything?" Mafan asked of her as soon as she entered the office.

From her reticule Aera pulled a portable pad and turned it on. She scrolled through a menu and then enlarged a specific electronic document. "There are three ships sailing at dawn," she reported, handing the device to her father.

Mafan scanned the record and said, "Fine. You watch these two," he indicated on the flat surface. "They are bound for the East."

"I tell you we ought to start at one end of that port and search every ship!" Aera declared.

Mafan shook his head. "Aera, no captain is going to let us aboard with a crew of trafficked sailors!"

"Well," she countered. "You're a prominent businessperson in this town. Can't you get the constable or the judge to issue a search warrant?"

"And take a chance they'd dump Neb and the others into the river before we could get to any of them?"

"Father," Narrtrok said emphatically. "There's another way. Let me go down to *Briny Red's* and get myself abducted."

"No, Son."

"But at least we'd know where Neb and the others are!"

"The only thing we'd know is that you'd all had been trafficked."

"You can follow me!"

"Narrtrok, these people are good at this game. They've been at it a long time!" Mafan stifled from shouting. His ire was rising, matching his children's frustration. "You think they are just going to drag you out the front door and make a public announcement?! Believe me, we'd lose all of you!" He sighed, then added, "No, we may have to take that gamble. Just not yet."

Silence filled the office. Along with it was the loneliness of a loved one missing.

"Just give me some more time," Mafan eventually said. "Briny Red is coming to the Ranch for lunch. There is still that angle."

Caelia had picked out one of her finest gowns to wear for her anticipated luncheon at the Mafan's estate. She had just secured the back fastenings when she her a 'splash' coming from her bathroom. Opening the portal, she found lounging in her voluptuous bathing tub one very nude Daviad Ayden. Luckily for her vision, most of his languid body was covered in soapy bubbles.

"Ahhh, Red, my love," he crooned.

"Daviad!" she scolded. "Why didn't you let me know you were in there?!"

"I thought it would be a pleasant surprise," he smiled ruefully.

Her reaction was to turn back into the bedroom and finish dressing.

"Since when do I need an invitation to my own place?" Ayden asked, rising from the tub and reaching for a nearby towel. Drying himself off, he procured his robe from a threshold hook and ventured into the bedroom after Caelia.

He stopped and embraced her from behind, taking a deep breath. "Awww, you are a sweet smelling one," he flattered. "I was out to the 'cold storage' mill in the highlands. There were only three fish on ice in there to add to the two I deposited."

"It was a slow night," Caelia explained, pulling away from him and opening her jewelry box on the dressing table. "It was the best I could do."

Ayden reach out and grabbed her by the nearest elbow and swung her around. "Well then, you're just going to have to try a little harder," he said. "I've got three captains waiting on crews."

"You've got six other places up and down the river," she reminded him. "Are they delivering any better than me?"

"No," he cooed, moving closer to her. "You're special, Red. You always were. Ever since the first time I laid eyes on you." Aryden's pupils dilated and the room filled with pheromones. His excitement for her was evident and he leaned forward to kiss her neck.

Coyly, she pushed from him and turned to finish with her cosmetic accoutrements. Aryden took notice and asked, "Hey, were you going dressed up like that?"

"I've been invited to lunch by a prominent local family," she explained, placing bedazzled earbobs on each of her two lughole lobes.

Aryden did his best to contain his laughter, but it still spilled out as he tried to question her more. "A local prom... in...ent ... family? What's *his* name?!" He restrained himself to add, "And during lunch what are you going to talk about?"

Caelia sighed, then huffed.

"Let's see," Aryden teased. "The price of a barrel of whiskey? Or the time that I found you hustling drinks in Laera Maesin."

He could see that she wasn't taking too kindly to his razzing, so he stopped and touched her arm affectionately. "Awww, Red, maybe old Daviad isn't the most handsome male on Un or the richest, yet. But we haven't done too badly have we, Love?" Then his eyes lit up and he dashed back into the bathing room. "Ohhh, I've got something for you!"

While he was out of the room, Caelia moved over to the bed where she had laid down the nosegay from Mafan. Picking it up, she had a moment of fancy until Aryden came back with a golden lame' box with an oversize pink ribbon and bow.

"Here you go," Aryden shoved the box into her hands, replacing the small bouquet of flowers. "This will make you forget that prominent local family. What's *he* got that old Daviad can't give ya!" He hurriedly helped unwrap the ribbon, bow, and box cover. "Go ahead. Take it out!" he told her, indicating the mound of tissue paper.

Lifting from the folds of thin gift wrapping was the pelt of some animal. She held it in her hands for just a moment before her revulsion for the dead animal hide had her bursting into tears and running from the apartment.

Aryden was flabbergasted.

"What? If you don't like the color, I can get you another one," he called after her. "Fine. I'll take it back, then!"

\*\*\*

Arhun swam hard and swam fast back to his family crèche, excited with what he had discovered this day, but knowing he could never share the experience with anyone. Lost in his reflections of the handsome Caecilian he did not notice the distinct rows of different plants beneath him, all growing together, but neatly spaced among themselves. There was no crowding, no competition for light or sandy soil among the green, pink, and amber vegetables.

Climbing over low sand dunes, the garden appeared to thicken in the distance. A few kicks brought Arhun to the growths. Wordless, he examined the unmissable signs of hand planting, constant weeding and care. He swam to the top of the first dune. He gently nudged through the dense vegetation crowning its top and studied the view beyond.

The farm stretched out impressively, occupying the sandy plain in all directions for a considerable distance. Far more commanding, however, were the shapes that swam slowly and purposefully among the intricate patterns.

The bipedal amphibian forms were akin to himself. Their skin was as radiant as his, a variant of the omnipresent amber, with shades of gold and green, while strands of vestigial hair the color of silver and gold tinsel topped their skulls. The females mixed in about equal numbers with males in the garden. Both genders were nude, yet the pigments in their integument reflected minute, metallic colors like that of shells arranged in a multitude of individual patterns.

He had been spotted. Several heads had turned to stare in his direction. Some of the figures were moving hastily forward, giving signs of irritation. He was in trouble for sure. He had been late to begin the harvest for mid-meal. Grinning coyly, Arhun floated up from his observation spot and shrugged as his guardians approached.

"Sorry, I am late," he apologized. "I got distracted, again."

***

Aera was indignant. She placed her hands on her hips and glared at her father in deviance. "I don't know how you expect us to sit and make polite conversation with that female," she proclaimed.

"That *female*, Aera," Dajal spoke as she rose from a parlor chair and moved closer to her daughter, "knows where Neb and the other males are located. We don't."

Collecting her runaway emotions, Aera signed and asked, "Well, what do you talk about with someone like Briny Red?"

"She is undoubtedly more worried about what she is going to say to us," Mafan counseled his daughter. In the distance, the subtle whine of a transport's hover engine could be heard approaching the front of the mansion. "She's here."

From one of the ventral bay windows, the three Mafans observed the female form within the hovercraft that stopped before the main house's front door. Her silhouette hesitated for a moment, the engine of the craft still purring. It seemed as if she was shaking her head; then the craft accelerated in a sharp turn back toward the primary gate of the property.

"'Roban," Dajal gasped. "She's driving away!"

"Ohhh," Aera exclaimed. "Father, go get her! Hurry!"

Mafan paused, thought before he said, "No. It won't work here. I can see that."

"Then what are we going to do?" Aera asked in a defeated tone.

"If she will not come into our world," Mafan said emphatically, "then I've got to go back to hers."

## CHAPTER SEVEN:

For several moments while Arhun floated in dark coolness, he saw nothing. Then he became aware that he could make out the familiar outlines of the trench around him, albeit dimly. Illumination emanated from close ahead. A few kicks brought him into increased light from overhead once again. Eventually he reached the end of the trench. Here the coral rampart dropped off in a steep cliff to a broad sandy plain deeper and wider than the one he'd just left. What rose lofty and ethereal there made the manicured gardens and jeweled schools of fish he'd passed through pale to insignificance.

He had arrived at this crèche's underwater settlement. Constructed with complete disregard for any ancient cataclysm, any present currents, and any concern of any sort save aesthetics. A metropolis of fancy.

Thin winding towers emulated the internal configuration of spiral seashells in grace and strength. Another huge, conchae-shaped structure dominated the city, rising in its center. It was as if the citadel had been poured whole, entire, from a single, carefully sculpted mold, instead of being built by piece and bit.

At the point nearest the base of the coral cliff, a large archway formed a prominent break in the wall that surrounded the city. Inhabitants were swimming in and out in a steady two-way stream, intent on unknown aspects of Un commerce.

He made rapid progress, keeping close to the walls of low-lying structures wherever feasible. Once he almost kicked head-on into a crowd of busy Mer as they stumbled into a central crossway. He had to dart back into a nook between buildings and wait for the pedestrians to pass. He was floating on the opposite side of a broad, open plaza from the huge shell-shaped central structure. Right now it was devoid of strollers, and he did not wonder at the absence of citizens. It was time for communal eating, and he was late. His parents would be furious if his seat was once again vacant at the clan dining table.

Quickly, Arhun swam across the plaza and took access to the palace via a side turret's archway. He entered twisting, winding halls.

The architecture had shucked off enough of the land-based memory to build without regard to the needs to overcome gravity – no staircases, no ladders, just smooth ramps and open spaces. Some of the passageways dipped up in curves, others ran down to undisclosed depths at crazy angles.

Swimming as fast and as quickly as his webbed hands and feet could propel him up and into a huge auditorium space near the roof of the palace, the main gathering hall. The palace, was like the majority of the structures in the underwater city, arranged with transparent or translucent roofs to let in the tri-light of the system's stars by day and moonlight of several small satellites that shared Un's orbit during the night.

Mass movement overhead would not only be disconcerting, it would block the light as well as eliminate privacy.

The hall's walls were decorated with huge globes of a creamy, pearlesque luster. A raised dais at the far end of the chamber was Arhun's destination. Its carved seats ringed around an opulent table set for dining were occupied by members of his clan.

He arrived just in time to hear his father's proclamation of thanks to the water gods for providing such a bountiful feast. As inconspicuously as he could, Arhun shifted into his place at the long table and exhaled just as the first course was placed before him by one of the many serving staff members. There were times like these that Arhun truly disliked being a member of the royal family.

***

The determined knock that came at Caelia's apartment's door startled her out of her shocked state of mind. She jumped. Then said, "Come in."

V'Quorgroban Mafan strolled determinedly inside, closing the door behind him. For a moment, he looked at her, trying to read her emotions from where she sat on her bed, head tilted low.

"I couldn't make it for lunch," she eventually said. "Something came up."

"Liar." Mafan calmly stated, then moved to sit beside her. "You were afraid to come in the house, weren't you?" He tilted his head and looked at her. "Huh-uh. I tell you what I am going to do. I will give you another chance." He leaned in close to her field of vision. "Have dinner with me."

"Not at your house," Caelia said.

"No. No. No. We will go out. To the best eatery in Baraze." Mafan paused for a moment, looking deeper into her eyes. "I want to prove something to you," he admitted. "About where you belong, Caelia."

She simply nodded, then shyly smiled.

When the champagne arrived, it was placed neatly into an awaiting stanchion's bucket of ice. Two full glasses were already in use. Mafan sipped while Caelia just stared nervously about.

"I feel like at any moment someone is going to throw me out of here," she confessed. "And, tell me to go back to the saloon where I belong."

"Caelia, no one is going to throw you out of here," Mafan said reassuringly. "You belong here, if you want too."

"Maybe tonight with you," she replied, flattered. "Just this once, for a laugh. I know who I am. I run a saloon. I may not be much to you. I'm not doing so badly."

Mafan nodded but looked downcast. "It is bad. As your friend, I can tell you it's worse than bad."

"You don't understand…"

"Oh, yes, I do." Mafan smiled, paternal. "Look, Caelia, I am not the constable. You don't have to pretend with me that it's just a saloon. I've heard otherwise."

Indignation was growing in Caelia's eyes. She clenched her jaw and said, "All right! So, a couple of herders get themselves liquored up and if they disappear… so it's my fault? Just like before?"

"A couple of herders disappear?"

"I'm saying if! *If* they disappear!" Caelia's gaze locked fierce with Mafan's. "The waterfront is a tough place. Herders, sailors, wharf riffraff. They get boozed up. I entertain them. If they fall off the dock, they better know how to swim." Aggressively, she leaned in toward him. "Now. Tell me what you want from me?"

Mafan's face softened. "I want you to feel that the next time, you can step out of your hover carriage, come into my house, and be treated like the beautiful female that you really are…"

Nervously, Caelia suddenly stood up. "I have to go."

"Don't …"

"Now," she said clearly. "Please."

And with that, she was rushing out the diner's front door and into the cool night air.

*** 

It was a hard retelling the encounter back at his office. Even harder for Dajal to hear. She had accompanied Mafan into town just in case new information had been discovered about their son from Caelia.

"We had a lovely dinner," Mafan said. "We talked…"

"And?" she asked.

"Nothing."

"You are still certain she's involved?"

"Yes. Yes, I am. Only…"

"Only what?"

"Oh, nothing."

Dajal smiled and touched her spouse tenderly on his nearest arm. "She is a beautiful female," she said. "All the signs of healthy genetics to be passed into a new generation."

"Isn't she," Mafan agreed. "And, yes."

"And, you wish you weren't involved in this filthy mess. Hmmm?"

"I don't know. All this lying to her. Pretending. I cannot help but to feel dirty about it."

Narrtrok strode determined into the workspace still wearing his sailor disguise. "They're moving some males to a ship!" he announced.

"How did you find out?" Dajal asked.

"I have a source at the docks," Narrtrok smiled.

"When?" Mafan asked, rising from where he had been seated against his desk.

"Later. I don't know what ship," Narrtrok admitted. "Or where. But I do know it is tonight."

## CHAPTER EIGHT:

Neb Mafan had had enough of captivity and was truly discusted with the apathy for freedom from his fellow captives. Like prey to slaughter the males around him just languidly laid about, waiting for the inevitable.

"Come on! Come on!" he raged at them. "Haven't any of you any fight in you to get out of this place?"

"It won't do you any good," one of the newcomers told him. "I've been trafficked two times now. And I never heard of anybody breaking free."

"The crimps know their business," another chimed in. "Or they wouldn't be in it for so long."

"So, you just give it all up, right?!" Neb flared.

He stopped in his rant when he heard the *hrump* of machinery approaching. Quickly he darted to the barred window. Sure enough, a vehicle was approaching.

Dashing toward to the doorway, he stood stoic beside its frame waiting. It opened and two more unfortunates were tossed in the room followed by roughhousing thugs that put everyone at a distance from the portal, including Neb.

When the way was cleared, the dapperly dressed Daviad Ayden strolled in and waited for his presence to be recognized and known. He chuckled as Neb was cowed in with the others.

"All right now," Ayden announced. "Who is first? You'll be signing aboard to schooner *Halcyon*. Bound for the East through the Bethune Strait. A tropical voyage to an East Sea paradise."

"And you just expect us to *just* sign on?" Neb quipped.

"We cannot put you aboard without your signature," Ayden admitted with a 'click' of his mandible. "Or at least your mark. Why that would be illegal."

Laughter ran around through the gang of thugs. Ayden motioned for one in particular who held an active electronic tablet to move forward.

"Sign the book," Ayden instructed the captives.

A newcomer that was positioned beside Neb went to move, he tried to restrain him but the male broke free of his hold and approached the illuminated square. One by one the newcomers filed in line behind and willingly complied with the order. Neb and Izagfor and Sonav remained together and motionless. Defiant. They stared at each other and then the others in amazement.

Ayden took notice and approached the two ranch workers, saying, "Don't be heroes, lads. Sign. The trip will be educational, and the work will make a true male of ya."

"Like them," Izagfor sneered at the newcomers.

"Oh, they've learned their lesson well," Ayden smiled. "Like I said, the trip is educational." Turning to an underling, he ordered. "Give him his first lesson."

Without pause, the stooge revealed a baton and began beating Izagfor heavily with it across the head, shoulders, and back. Neb was instantly to his feet and rushing in to save his worker. His path was intervened by another of Ayden's males that tackled Neb to the floor, knocking the wind out of him. Gasping for breath, Neb noticed he was lying beside his fallen employee. Izagfor did not look well. He'd gone unnaturally pale and still. So very still. His eyes were opened, but fixed and unresponsive. The life had been literally been knocked out of him. A pool of blood lay under Izagfor's temple.

"He's dead!" Neb screamed in horror. "He's dead you murderers!"

Two armed lackeys dragged Neb away from the still form of Izagfor while a clean-up crew of more minions dragged his lifeless body from the room. In moments a hard splash could be heard in the distance of something heavy hitting the river below from a great altitude.

Ayden stepped forward and got close to Sonav's face. "Are you ready to sign now?" he asked arrogantly and unruffled.

Before he did anything, Sonav looked toward Neb for guidance. Relenting, he nodded, and the rancher placed his palm on the lighted membrane of the tablet. After his print was scanned, Sonav stepped back numb.

Ayden looked expectantly at Neb as the tablet was placed, under armed guard, in front of him. This would be a shotgun coercion. Neb did his palm scan, but he never took his hateful gaze from a delighted Ayden.

With the business at hand finished, Ayden and his crew stepped toward the door. "Congratulations, Lads. You just signed on with the toughest male to ever captain a ship. You guessed it, Lads, which would be Ifan Kold! Well, beautiful voyage!"

With that, Ayden and his followers made a speedy exit, locking the portal behind them. The tension in the air remained. All those left behind looked shell-shocked at one another. None of them ever expected such violence to lead to another's death. The vileness of the action permeated the air, they could taste the lingering bitterness of death.

As for Neb, he knew the proper time to mourn his worker's death would come. For now, he obsessed over the captain's name. Kold. He approached the newcomer that he had first spoken with before Ayden's signing shame.

"Kold," he said to him. "Would that be *the* Captain Ifan Kold?"

"The same," the male nodded, almost winching. "No crueler captain on the seas. Twelve lashes from a cat-of-nine, raises a hundred and eight welts on a bare back. His first mate, Conr uses it every single day."

"I have met the male," Neb confessed. "At a party. At my father's house."

"You think he'd help us?"

"We're not out to sea, yet," Neb smiled, hopeful.

Caelia had changed out of her gown into her usual 'work dress' just as a knock came at her apartment's door. She was in no mood to entertain.

"Go away!" she demanded.

The knocking continued. Whomever it was, they were not going to comply. Angrily, she marched to the door and slid it open, face set to bark at the begetter of the rapping on the panel. It was 'Roban Mafan.

"Caelia," he said.

"'Roban."

"I've got something I want to say," Mafan declared walking fully into the loft.

"You cannot stay, 'Roban…"

"I've got something on my mind ever since dinner…"

"'Roban, I am expecting someone."

"Well, whoever it is, he'll just have to wait."

Caelia rushed up to stare him in the face. "I thought we'd said our goodbyes!"

"That's just the point, Caelia," Mafan sighed. His eyes softened. "I want it to stay a good night, not a goodbye. You're going to have to make a choice. And, right now. This night."

"A choice?" her voice softened.

"A choice between this life here," he said to her. His demeanor wholly truthful. "Or a life in my part of town."

"I don't know what you're talking about."

"Listen to me," Mafan took her nearest arm. "I am asking you to give it up. All of it. And, I am not talking about just the saloon. I mean the crimping."

She pulled away, "Let me go…"

"The trafficking," Mafan followed after her. "Don't bother to lie about it, Caelia. You practically admit it that three herders were trafficked out of this place last night. You're in it up to your neck!"

"'Roban, please," she pleaded. "You've got to get out of here! Now, I told you I was expecting someone!"

"Give it up, Caelia." Now it was Mafan that was pleaded. "You are better than this. Believe me you are. Walk away. If you don't, there will never be a chance for you to become a member of my clan. I have two eligible sons. Together with one of them, your choice. I want that chance for you."

Indecision rippled across her pretty countenance. Her eyes flickered in doubt. A million synapses fired behind them as which path to take.

"You can start this night," Mafan continued. "Release those three herders. Now."

"I cannot do that."

"Then, tell me where they are."

The door panel slid opened and allowed Daviad Ayden entrance. He spotted the close tableau and his viridescent expression darkened. "Well," he hissed. "I do not believe I have had the pleasure."

Mafan stepped away from Caelia and faced the other male fully. Bowed slightly in polite gentleman fashion and introduced himself. "V'Quorgroban Mafan," he said.

"Daviad Ayden. You a friend of Red's?"

"Yes. And, we were just about to leave," Mafan turned to Caelia. He looked at her, imploringly. "Weren't we, Caelia?"

"Oh, '*weren't we, Caelia*'." Ayden mocked. Over his shoulder, he shouted, "Jael! Rafel!"

Two armed thugs quickly filled the opening doorframe, taking positions on opposite sides of Ayden. Their dirty faces worn with the years of illicit living. Their intentions evident.

Softly, Caelia stepped between them and said, "I think you better go, 'Roban."

Mafan touched her shoulder and said sincerely, "Caelia, this is your last chance. Make the right choice."

Ayden had seen and heard enough. Charging forward like an enraged lover, he grabbed Mafan by a shoulder and slung him head-first into the swinging batons of his two subordinates. Their blows landed in vital areas on the male's body, but that did not stop him for defending himself. One lackey felled to the floor from a nicely placed right-hook fist. The other doubled over from a left jab to the abdomen. In the end it did no good for Mafan, the first recovered quickly and placed a successful hit behind Mafan's neck plexus, knocking him unconscious in one swoop.

"If you traffick him," shouted Caelia. "Daviad, we are through. I mean it, Daviad!"

Whether it was her tone, her rigid stance, or her clenched fists, she would never know what had swayed Ayden to instruct his two aides to dump Mafan's body in the alley. But, she was grateful.

"You're going back to Laera Maesin with me," Ayden declared. "This night. Just as soon as I hand Kold his crew."

"Daviad, I want to quit."

"Quit, huh?" Ayden scoffed. "For him?! That fancy trousers? That Mafan?! You're stupid! What has he been telling you?!" He was shouting, but not out of pure anger. There was something else in his tone... desperation? Love? Something even he wasn't quite ready to tell her. "And, how stupid are you to believe him? He is.... Mafan..." Ayden suddenly stopped. His recent memory stirring. "Mafan. Mafan. That name is familiar. Now who is he? What does he ..." He looked Caelia squarely in the face. His eyes sparkling with thoughts connecting. "Does he know about our operation here?!" he asked.

"No!"

"Are you sure?" Ayden growled. "Tell me fast. Cause if you are lying to me, I'll..."

"I am just trying to make friends in the right part of town," Caelia said. "That's what you want me to do, isn't it? Butter up the *right* people?!"

Ayden's face went still. "I pray that you are not lying to me," he simply replied. *"Cae-li-a."* He emphasized each part of her proper name.

## CHAPTER NINE:

Constable Ryder Thoms was not happy. He paced the Mafan Company's main office around all those assembled. From the CEO to his spouse and gathered remaining children.

"'Roban, you went about this all wrong," he chided. "You should have come to me in the first place!"

"Well, while we are sitting here pointing digits, my son, Neb maybe shipped off to the gods knows to where!" Dajal cried out.

"That's why if had come to me sooner…"

"My son's life is a stake!" she shouted. "We did what we thought was the best! And, we'd do it the same way again!"

"Ryder, you're just wasting time!" Mafan interjected.

Thoms directed his next statement toward Narrtrok. "Are you sure you want to go through with it?" he asked.

"Ryder! For the love of…" Mafan called out.

"All right!" the constable cut him off. "I said, the plan has a chance of working. Now, I have got to tell you I think Narrtrok has a chance of winding up dead if it doesn't."

"I'll take that chance," the youth said.

Nodding, Thoms said as he headed for the office's door, "I'll round up some deputies."

Then he was gone.

Mafan poured some libation from a decanter on his desk into an empty crystal glass and handed it to his son. "To give you a head start," he smiled proud. And, then splashed it over Narrtrok's tunic. With a pat on the shoulder, he gave him permission to leave.

Without a backward glance, Narrtrok gathered his cast aside pea coat and exited. It was only a short walk from the company headquarters through the main village square to get to the docks. As he approached his destination, he altered his gait to be more staggered until he was practically leaning on the bar counter at *Briny Red's* for support, banging on the wooden top demanding liquor.

"Barkeep!" he slurred. "I want more to drink! I'm an ole sea wolf of a male And, I like to howl all night long! I want whiskey! Whiskey!"

Narrtork's outlandish behavior had caught the attention of Rebexa. And, she quickly took advantage of the impaired sailor. Summoning both Red and Ayden from the upstairs apartment, she beckoned, "We have a likely *fish* downstairs." As they joined her on the balcony overlooking the bar area, she asked, "Should we hook him?"

Ayden laughed and nodded. "Kold will take all that we bring. He needs a full crew."

Rebexa did what she did best. Seduction. And within heartbeats she had descended the stairs and captured the wandering attentions of the drunken sailor. "What will it be?" she breathed heavily.

"Well, anything as long as it ain't water," Narrtrok stumbled.

"Oh, it won't be water," Rebexa chuckled, heading to the bar.

Red moved in to distract the marine by offering to dance with him while the bartender and Rebexa 'spiked' a drink. Ayden moved in to watch the whole operation. He suddenly had doubts about his key player.

Alluringly, Red moved closer and placed her lips next to the male's closest lughole, whispering, "You've got to get out of here, now!" she pleaded.

"Aaalllrright, honeybee, if you don't want to daannceee," Narrtrok continued his act. "Then, then let's …"

"…have a drink," Red finished the statement, feeling Ayden's gaze burning into her. She escorted the staggering male over to where Rebexa waited with the tainted glass of whiskey.

"You are the prettiest thing I've ever seen," Narrtrok complimented.

Ayden's stares were getting more severe.

"Well, then, why…um… don't you have a drink," Red offered.

Narrtrok leaned against her for support, feigning exhaustion. "Is there a place on this transport where a mate can lie down?" he giggled, sleepily. Then he quietly snored.

Ayden rushed over and took the limp body off of Red and ushered it into the PRIVATE back room, saying, "Ahhh, this way to the sleeping car, Mate."

Red followed. She wasn't sure why. *To see to the safety of the stranger?*

Had Mafan's word finally gotten through the layers of survival? Could she do better than this life?

Ayden deposited the sleeping sailor in the back of a flatbed transport in the alley behind the saloon. Moving to the operations chair, he called after her, "Come on, Red. I want you where I can keep an eye on you!"

Drowsily, she followed. Taking the passenger seat in the forward compartment. Ayden sat behind the driving mechanisms and activated the small vehicle's engine. Shifting the gears into driving mode, he accelerated the craft forward.

Unknown to them both, their movements were under surveillance. Mafan joined the squadron of deputies and the constable on lev-cycles and closely followed the receding image of Ayden's flatbed out of the town proper and up into the highlands.

Neb Mafan had just drifted off into some well needed sleep when he was aroused by the barking of orders from Ayden's ruffians. "All right, you lot! On your feet!" he said. "Captain Kold wants to look over his new crew!"

One by one, the captives rose as a silhouetted figure emerged from the dark night into the wan lighting of the mill's basement. The newcomer Neb had befriended lean close to them as they filed into a line, saying, "That's Kold. If you know him, now is your chance to say something."

Captain Kold was typical of sea males that had been at sea for far too long. A shriveled creature, hardy in stature though walked with a cane. He looked as though only a gale wind could blow him down. The old male's deep wrinkles seemed to carve a map of his life on his still agile and mobile facial features. An iron will brewed within. Seen through the eyes; like looking into the percolations of a cauldron. He was dressed in his full captain's uniform, slightly tattered though it was.

"Good evening, Males," he addressed the line. "I hope you are all well." When he got to the end, the male he faced looked vaguely familiar.

"Captain Kold, I am Neb Mafan."

The familiarity hit with brutal clarity and Kold flinched. His expression hardened and he looked to his escorts. "Let this male out," he ordered. "I want to talk to him."

The captain and his crew moved Neb out the door and up the basement stairs to the outside. The night air was damp and bracing, a chill that set deep into the bones. Standing beside some shrubbery,

Kold turned to Neb and said, "This is most unfortunate, Neb Mafan."

"All right, all right," Neb said, holding back his temper. "Straighten out, will you, Captain?"

"I am sorry. There is nothing I can do."

"Nothing?!" Neb was appalled. "We were abducted. One of my males was killed."

Kold turned to one of his crew and asked, "Bring me the ship's articles."

The sailor withdrew a tablet from his messenger bag he had slung from one shoulder over to cross to hang by the opposite hip. Activating the electronic device, he called up the requested documents. Reading over the script, Kold asked, "Neb Mafan, is this not your palm signature?"

"We were forced to sign," Neb explained. "One of my males was beaten to death because he didn't."

Kold looked to one of Ayden's males in the small group that crowded around them. "That's not true, Captain," the male said. "They all signed of their own free will."

"Was someone beaten?"

"No. One male deserted, but I don't think will ever see him again." The male smiled at the captain, then looked meaningfully at Neb. "He wouldn't want to face a court-martial for desertion, now would he, Captain?"

Neb had heard enough and moved to act. Kold called out and stopped him mid-way, "Mafan! You are under my command. Your very life for the next two years is in my hands. From now on, you will not speak to me without my prior permission. Is that understood?"

Neb clenched his teeth. He knew he was trapped.

"Lock him up," Captain Kold instructed. "We sail at dawn."

The posse rode fast behind the fading darken outline of the flatbed. A winding path led far up into the highlands, along a cliff ridge overlooking the Douro River and to an old mill. The flatbed arrived and quickly deposited its cargo, unawares they had a tail.

Neb was surprised, but happy to see the form of his youngest brother when it had been brought into the holding room. Concern washed away as Narrtrok opened his clear eyes and winked at him. A rescue plan was in play.

Outside, Ayden and Kold conducted business.

"The currency is all there, I assure you," the captain said, tapping his transference card to the other's mobile data device (MDD). "I'm an honest male."

"We're all honest, Captain," Ayden replied. "We stay honest by not trusting anybody."

Constable Thom and his deputies along with Mafan had parked their lev-cycles behind the outlying support buildings to the mill and quietly walked up to observe the transaction, hiding behind old supply wagons. A surprise came when Caelia started the flatbed up unexpectedly.

Ayden rushed over and grabbed the steering yoke. "Where do you think you're going?!"

"Back to town," she declared loudly. "I am finished with this business!"

"Oh, you're finished, are you?" Ayden hissed. "Then I should have taken care of your fancy pimp after all, huh?" He paused, then growled. "And, I thought I had smartened you up some. You didn't really think I'd let you go, did you? And, if you ran, you'd known I'd have come after you." He deactivated the engine and turned to his closest roughneck and ordered, "Keep a close eye on her and make sure she doesn't go anywhere." Turning to the rest of his lout, he ordered, "All right, let's get them up and loaded."

While Red was under watch by the one ruffian, Ayden and two others went into the mill's basement to retrieve the captives. When they entered the room, Ayden ordered them to form a single line against the nearest wall to the door.

"We're going for a little ride," he joked. He noticed the newest arrival was still laying side-lying on the floor. "Pick him up," he told one of the two rogues that had accompanied him in.

As the hooligan moved to rouse the sleeping figure with his foot, Narrtork grabbed it and twisted onto his back, taking the male with him. Both sprawled on the floor, Narrtrok pinning the other down. A gun when flying and into the hands of Neb, who promptly aimed it at Ayden's head. Marching forward, he put the ringleader into a choke-hold and ordered, "Now, you yell out to the remaining males of yours and tell them to unlock and open this door or I'm going to put a hole right through your head!" Ayden struggled, remaining quiet. "Tell them, or I'll blow you apart!"

Ayden relaxed and capitulated. "Open up," he hollered. "We're coming out."

As soon as the portal opened, chaos reigned. Pushing and shoving to get outside from the captives. Hearing the commotion, Constable Thom and his entourage made their advance. Ayden's cortege recognized the deputies' uniforms and opened fire on the moving posse. Kold and his crew vanished into the ebon night. Each running for cover, a few falling on both sides from energy pulse wounds.

Ayden had made his way outside and was hiding behind a grouping of barrels. In desperation, he called out, "Red, back the flatbed here!"

Caelia had been laying down on the front compartment's two bucket seats when the firing had started. Her watcher was one of the first to fall. She heard the cry of her lover and instinct took over. She activated the engine, but before she could put the driving gears in reverse motion, Roban Mafan was in the cabin and struggling to keep her from moving the vehicle.

"What are you doing?!" she insisted, struggling against the large male's grip on her arms. "You tricked me! How could you do that to me?!"

"My two sons are in there!" Mafan shouted.

"Everything you said!" she cried, twisting about until she fell from the vehicle onto the sandy dirt. "You're a liar!"

Ayden took the distraction as an opportunity and dashed for the idle vehicle. Shifting it into forward gear and moving the acceleration lever forward. As the craft moved in an arc to clear the buildings, Mafan took the driver into his gun's sights and fired. An energized bullet of light struck Ayden square between his shoulder blades and he slumped. The craft hovered in inactive mode, its driver's body followed inertia and continued to slip from the driver's seat out and onto the ground.

Caelia rushed to his fallen side. "Daviad!" she cried out.

The shooting had stopped. The constable's auxiliary had taken into custody anyone left alive from the trafficking party while freeing the captives. Mafan went to stand over kneeling Caelia and her deceased lover. She looked up at him after she had rolled Ayden's lifeless body onto its back. There was no doubt. Her jailer was gone. The expression on her face was that of a female scorned.

"You used me," she sobbed. "All my life, males have used me."

Mafan had nothing to say. His emotions in a mixer. There were no words. His focus had to be his family. Turning he embraced his two sons as they ran to him. While they celebrated their joy of reuniting, the whimpers of a disdained heart breaking resounded on the cool aura of the night. Specters were walking amongst them.

## CHAPTER TEN:

With all the breath he could muster, Neb Mafan blew out the candles on his birthing cake with zeal. The dining room was once again decorated in celebration of his day. Family and friends formed a circle around the main eating table filled with cutlery, finery, food, and in the center of it all an elaborate cake smothered in confectionary icing. Applause followed as the last of the candles were extinguished.

"Well I hope none of you are planning on eating any of this," Neb joked. "Because I am planning on eating all of this myself!"

"Yeah, yeah," Aera teased. "I want an end piece."

Narrtrok joined in with his mother and laughed. "We each want a piece as well," he said. "The one with the big flower on it!"

Obliging, Neb began cutting up the gateau in equal sections with a serving spatula. While the dividing of the soft, sweet food made from a mixture of flour, shortening, eggs, sugar was placed on plates and handed out to each of the guests and family members, Mafan stood aside from the festivities in deep thought.

Being a sensitive son, Narrtrok took notice of his father's melancholy and moved to stand beside him. "Where are your thoughts this day?" he asked.

Mafan smiled. "At the jail," he simply answered.

"You still think of her?"

"She's going to need good representation at her trial. Character witnesses."

"In that department, she'll have the best that there is," Narrtrok smiled, offering him a plate of cake.

Each smiled at the other, then took a respective forkful of confectionary and ate it with delicious enjoyment. When they had finished eating, Mafan returned to the warmth of the partygoers while Narrtrok ventured outside to the estate's boathouse for a long-anticipated rendezvous. He had someone very special to thank for providing not only information that led to his younger brother's rescue, but also for awakening something deep within that could no longer be suppressed.

They found each other in the folds under a suspended rowboat. The boathouse was a building especially designed for the storage of boats, normally smaller craft such as punts or small motorboats for sports or leisure use. Typical, it was located on open water, a tributary of the Douro River.

"There you are! How are you?" asked Narrtrok of the other. He smelled of saline and musk, fresh and new as when the world was new.

"Come closer and find out for yourself," taunted Arhun, reaching out and wrapping his arms around a solid torso. There was a moistness to him.

Parting after a lingering kiss, Narrtrok sighed content. "Can't sleep either, huh?" he joked.

"No." Arhun was suddenly serious. "It has between 4 and 7 hours since I've been submerged. I'll have to return to the water soon."

"Understood."

Arhun frowned, lowering his head in sadness.

"Now, we talked about this," Narrtrok reminded. "No reason to get crazy over this situation."

"Fine. I need to…"

"*Shhh*, just take a moment. It's going to be what it's going to be."

Arhun nodded, collected his thoughts. Lifting his elfin countenance, he looked directly into

Narrtrok's gaze. "What are you thinking about right now?" he asked.

"Good times. Hard times. It's been an unforgettable few hours."

"I hope I can be the kind of distraction that can help you relax," Arhun nuzzled closer to Narrtrok, seeking reassurance and comfort. Perhaps even something else, something deeper. "Relaxing will help you focus."

As one they each leaned into the other and kissed. The link continued, quickly evolving into Narrtrok's clothing being removed and Arhun once again on his back, fitting nicely in the curve of the watercraft. As before, they rolled about kissing, hugging, massaging, and joining as one.

When their lovemaking was finished, their afterglow lasted well into the early morning. Each made drowsy by the security of the other's presence. Falling asleep in their mutual embrace came quickly. There they stayed until a weak and watery dawn roused them, moisture and dim light seeping through the cracks of the boathouse roof and walls. Arhun found Narrtrok nude as a needle sitting pensive on the dinghy's edge.

"What is it?" the mermale asked concerned, rising to sit behind him, his chin roosting comfortably on the other male's shoulder. Enjoying their bare bodies pressed against each other, feeling so natural in the contact.

Their combined body heat shivered off the morning chill.

"Are we going to make it, Arhun?"

"We're ready," the smaller male reassured, wrapping his smaller arms around the expansive breadth of his partner's upper torso. "We've come together with the vision that we can build the hope of uniting our two peoples."

"Well, I am glad I can inspire that in you," Narrtrok smiled. "Sometimes …." He stopped, turned, and gently caressed his lover's nearest cheek. "You are right, give us hope and a fighting chance…. yeah… anyone who opposes us better watch themselves."

"Absolutely," Arhun cheered. "Bring it on."

"Your people, your family… your *father*?"

"I know the consequences."

"And, I am going to fight for the right to hold you." Narrtrok took his beloved mermale into his arms and never shifted his eyes from his, adding, "And, know that I love you, always."

"I love you too."

"Although we will have many challenges ahead of us," Narrtrok affirmed. "We can face them together."

# Para

## TERENO

### CHAPTER ONE:

All year round, the world of Para's flora and fauna were full of surprises. From the southern Austere Mountains to one of the largest swamp regions on the planet from the stark country of Sasse to the desert-like dunes of the Kalifornio Coast. A world with enough space for unique wildlife, cultivated landscapes, and people who fostered old traditions.

In pockets, life was simple. Those still living off the land had learned to adapt. For a world with economic aspirations, some parts of Para seemed to have been trapped in a time warp. Some people still followed ancient traditions.

The municipality of Salo Ebena was situated amidst the farmland of the Granda Valo, a sub-region of the Central Valley. In and around the city proper were thousands of miles of waterways, which made up the Kalifornio Delta. When settlers first visited the Salo area, it was occupied by the Cumne, a branch of the Northern Valley Okuts Amerinds. They built their villages on low mounds to keep their homes above regular floods. The Siskiou Trail began in the northern Granda Valo. It was a centuries-old Amerind footpath that led through the Central Valley over the Cascade Sierras and into present-day Oregana.

Surrounded by open, angular hardscrabble landscape shaped by erosion from rain and wind. A densely packed salt pan, a dried-up desert lake. Formed in a closed hollow where rainfall could not drain away. Unlike in a wet climate where a lake would form, in a desert the water was heated and evaporated into vapor faster than it could be replenished by rain. The salt and minerals dissolved in the water left behind as a solid layer, shining pink under the red sun.

The winter's torpor had ended. Major waterways flowed again, despite the tenacity of ice and frost. Huge quantities of meltwater caused lowland rivers to overflow their banks. Large swathes becoming half water, half land; wild and untamed. Colorful blooms heralded a rapid warming trend. Ornithological migrations ensued. Salo Ebena's seaport served as a gateway to the Central Valley and beyond. It provided easy access for trade and transportation to the southern thurbidian crystal mines. Natives from all over the local star systems had arrived in the area on their way to the crystal fields. The city had grown rapidly as a miners supply point during the Crystal Fury. Consequently, it developed as a river port, the hub of roads to the thurbidian settlements in the Granda Valo and northern terminus of the Vojo de Los-Anĝeleso.

Salo Ebena was a city with a concentric system of buildings and thoroughfares. Administration and government at its hub with social and utility services radiating out in the first ring, business and trades in the second, followed by live-work residential complexes, schools, and recycling water plants in the third and fourth districts, ending at the city's fringe with family homes, estates, and satellite depots for power, sewage, and long-distant transport.

In a clustered district was one of several Land Transport Authority (LTA) stations peppered across the metropolis. Supporting service businesses circled around the transit polestar. A saloon, hostel lodging, and assembly point for the land shuttles resembled a small independent community. Despite state-of-the-art irrigation from underground wellsprings and the Delta feeding lush parks and hanging gardens, the true arid climate of the area was ever present.

The heat was unbearably oppressive for Emilie Lepid, a first generation tailless squamate immigrant from the planet Un, first from this star system's sun. A curious race whose integument anthropomorphic morphology gradually took shape, including traits such as well-developed optical nerve systems for tracking prey movement, tongues evolved to catch prey, and the incomplete but useful chemical sensory system, designed for olfactory, gustatory and food detection. Skin that was resplendent in its pigmentation, no two persons had alike, an achievement in and of itself.

Each Unling seemingly more attractive than the last. None of which were helping her dissipate the accumulating heat trapped in her stylish, yet heavy traveling clothes. Consisting of a simple gingham skirt with matching printed paisley blouse, cloned-leather boots and silken hosiery; fashionable yet not practical for the climate nor her species.

She leaned against the boarding porch's supporting stanchion for the overhang as she waited for the transport skimmer to finish having the passengers' luggage loaded. A dampen handkerchief her only solution for mopping up her perspiration.

Most of Emilie's species were distinguished by two rows of spots going down each side of their hairless bodies, from forehead to toe. Skin color could vary; at present, hers was abnormally pale.

Skimmer pilot Captain Charles Cross took notice of one of his passenger's discomfort, not only because of how distressed she appeared, but also because of her exotic, off-world beauty. His hair and beard dark, eyes and mouth hard. A male who believed that words were deeds. Timidly, he approached her, saying, "It will be an easier ride today." He smiled reassuringly with a lop-sided grin.

A hominid, Cross was a lean and muscled male approaching middle-age. Years of working as a transportation driver had honed not only his intuitive skills but also his physique. The sinew of his form moved statuesque under the tight lines of his uniform's shirt and trousers. By all accounts he would be considered handsome.

"It will be cooler once we get out of the flatlands," he added.

Emilie grinned in returned, asking, "How much longer before we disembark?"

"Just a couple of minutes." He noticed her baggage set aside on the boardwalk. "May I take this for you?"

"Yes, please."

Glad to have the connection and to be of service, Cross quickly picked up the compact tubular case by its worn handles and proceeded to the stern of the skimmer transport parked a few feet away. Platform stewards busied themselves about the craft as its support crew ran through pre-departure checks.

Anson Lamont was a typical drunken traveling marketer. Unkempt from his unruly hair to his wrinkled business suit, he epitomized a lost soul. Yet, he still had an eye for beauty. He had seen the interchange between Emilie and the captain the moment he had exited the town saloon, his senses pleasantly numbed by his latest ingestion of libation.

"Ready to go forward. You can board now, Sir Lamont," Cross instructed, seeing the peddler approach the skimmer. "We are ready to pull out."

"Thank you, Captain. I'm going to assist Sinjorino Lepid first."

Passing the captain as he placed one of Emilie's bags into the luggage compartment, Lamont nodded his head in a chivalries gesture toward the object of his observation while reaching out to take the last of her luggage.

"Morning, Sinjorino Lepid. Anson Lamont at your service."

"Thank you, but I can manage by myself," Emilie protested, following her pursuer as he turned toward the opened luggage bin.

"Now, Sinjorino Lepid," Lamont crooned, "we've been traveling a good many miles, it's time we were friends, don't you think?"

"If you'll excuse me, Sir Lamont," Emilie bullied her handbag away from the male and shouldered its strap.

Lamont blocked her way as she made for the side passenger hatch. "I noticed you went to bed early last night," he leered. "Now, in the next town I have a stay-over for a couple of days, why don't you and I …"

In his haste to impress upon the target of his desires, Lamont had failed to notice that the remaining complement of passengers had arrived and were watching his exchange with Emilie Lepid with annoyance, especially two prominent-looking humanoid males. The third observer was an older polished female of their species, dressed in tailored black cloned-leather skirted pants and matching blouse. These were three members of a much larger clan of a wealthy, influential family living in Salo Ebena's Central Valley. Euphemia Hille and two of her four sons, the elder Rikard, the younger Sano.

"Why don't you just back off Sir Lamont!" barked Rikard. "I don't think the lady is interested."

A barrister by trade, but a labor-hardened rancher, nonetheless. The manner of his walk and stance echoed Rikard was not to be taken as weak by the refined clothing he donned. His height was nearly the same as the mobile retailer, but his frame solid with chiseled muscle made obvious by the cut and molding of his traveling suit. There was no doubt the outcome of any confrontation between the two.

"Let's get aboard folks," ordered Captain Cross. He had seen enough of the exchange and knew when rising frustrations were turning for the worse.

With measured strides, each moved toward the passenger module's opened side hatch. Lamont avoided the stoic gazes from the Hille trio as he turned to join the queue.

The low whirl of a hovercycle interrupted everyone's focus. An octopod male who obviously had been riding in the desert for a considerable time straddled the purring motorbike as he guided it to a stop beside the waiting skimmer passengers.

"Excuse me," he called out to a landing steward. "East toward Oregana?"

"That's correct," Cross said.

"Well, I just came from that way. Back about ten miles in the Sawtooth Mountains, there's a rock side. A bad one. There isn't going to be anything but horse and foot trails for quite a while."

Cross swore under his breath. "Nothing's come through from Tower Control."

"It just happened," the stranger offered an explanation.

"What does that mean?" asked Euphemia Hille.

"We've got to use the old Siskiou Trail, Sinjorino Hille," the captain explained. "It cuts north through Black Rock." He frowned. "That'll get us into Oregana a day late." He turned to the messenger and smiled, grateful. "Thanks, friend."

"Right."

"We best get started," Cross said with a gesture to continue boarding.

Without delay, the skimmer's one-person crew ushered the skimmer's passenger into their pre-selected seats, harnessed them in, and took his jump-seat position while Captain Cross and his co-pilot sealed the shuttle and moved the controls to put the station-keeping engines to full throttle.

Without too much fanfare, Lieutenant Breck Bezzerides confirmed clearance from Tower Control with an alternative flight plan.

*"This is Tower Control to Route 935. You are cleared for departure."*

Bezzerides then gave Cross the 'go-ahead'. The oblong transport elevated fully from the dusty tarmac and quickly shot forward along its catapult and beyond the flight complex's perimeter without further delay.

The messenger stood quietly, smiling from the porch of the saloon along with two other males. Each worn in posture by hard work without much reward. All three from the same hominid sub-species, resembling various branches of the primate tree. But all had the same expression as the skimmer grew smaller and smaller as the horizon claimed it.

"Everything is fine," the messenger turned to the male at his right shoulder. "They believed everything I told them."

"So did Tower Control," the male replied.

With a nod, the two joined him as they walked toward their parked hovercycles.

## CHAPTER TWO:

Sano Hille found it odd that once the journey had begun, how quickly everyone on the skimmer had gone silent. A young male far from youth, but nowhere near middle-age, the handsome blonde-haired lad sat beside one of the passenger module's four window ports watching the landscape whisk by at over three hundred miles per hour. His mother sat directly to his right, pleasantly engaged in her hand-held tablet's presentation of the latest romance novel, while to her side rested the on-edge Emilie Lepid.

Across from Sano reclined his elder sibling, Rikard. An empty seat was between him and the ever-inebriated Lamont, who had more interest in the small flask in his right hand than the desertscape rushing by his left. His deep baritone voice suddenly spoke up and drowned out the underlying 'hum' of the elevation engine.

"Country like this," he said, finishing another swig, "Nothing. That's all. Nothing. Dead. All over dead. Makes me wonder why I travel these parts."

"Why do you travel these parts, Sir Lamont?" asked Euphemia, her stern eyes rising from the lip of her tablet to gaze at the male. "You haven't told us."

"I sell death, Sinjorino," Lamont said deadpan. "I travel dead country to help people get dead. Simple as that. I'm a hand weapons seller." He reached below his seat and pulled out of the bag caddy a square case, of which he promptly placed on his lap and undid its latches.

Lifting the lid, he added, "This lot, ten percent." The case held three pulse-energy pistols, each held in its own foam-formed niche. Seeing the others' stunned reaction, he smiled reassuring, saying, "They are not charged. Best of the line." He lifted an ivory-handed sharpshooter and went on with a pitch. "Precision made, hair-trigger, guaranteed."

"Guaranteed to… do what, Sir Lamont?" asked Emilie.

"Shoot straight. Kill whatever you shoot at if your aim is good."

Emilie returned his smile with a melancholy nod.

Sano took the proffered pistol and began to examine it. Lamont continued with his rehearsed script.

"It would look mighty fine in that holster of yours."

"I carry a weapon for protection," Sano replied with a meaningful look. "Mine will do just fine."

"Ain't no gun ever made was made to kill. Protection is just a nice way of putting it."

Sano became disenchanted with the pistol and moved to return it to Lamont, saying, "That's your way of looking at it."

Midway, the gesture was intercepted by Emilie. She grabbed the pistol from Sano.

"May I see that please?" she asked, gripping the gun by its smooth handle.

Sano released his grip and met his mother's watchful eye with his.

"That was not meant for ladies," Lamont stammered. "Ladies carry something lighter. Smaller. Easier to …"

He stopped his explanation when he realized that Emilie was pointing the pistol directly at him at point-blank range like an expert.

"Now… it's not a good idea to point guns, especially since it isn't loaded."

"Say it is loaded," Emilie said, oddly calm. "Right now. How do you like looking at death in the face, Sir Lamont?"

The male scoffed and tried to say, "Sinjorino…"

"You talk about death really easy," Emilie smirked. "Almost like it is a joke. Well, how do you like it? How do you feel?"

Without hesitation, she cocked the gun's firing chamber and took precise aim across the aisle. Everyone seemed to shift nervously in their seats.

"Just a slight pressure on the trigger," she seemed to narrate the obvious.

"Sinjorino…" Lamont tried to reason.

"The male that killed my spouse used one of these pistols," she explained eerily. "You could have been the male that sold it to him. Don't you find that amusing?"

Everyone sans Emilie seemed to jump when a distinctive 'click' ricocheted off the small cabin's polished bulkheads. She had simply pulled the pistol's trigger. Her hand holding the weapon then slumped to her side. Euphemia quickly took the gun into her gloved hands and handed it to Lamont silently, without ever taking her eyes off of Emilie.

"Well, I guess no one needs a new gun," Lamont said. "I will just put these away."

As the case closed and was returned to the underseat caddy, Rikard spoke up, saying, "I think that would be a good idea, Sir Lamont."

Euphemia leaned privately closer to Emilie and whispered, "I'm sorry about your spouse." She spoke from experience.

"It's over," Emilie exhaled.

A momentary silence returned to the module as the tension that had mounted slowly dissipated.

Dust settled. Boredom returned. Lamont took an alleviating gulp from his flask and lamented at the rushing landscape.

"Killer," he said, more to himself than the others. "That's what it is. Just lying out there waiting. Its saying: 'Come on. I won't hurt ya.' It'll cook ya to death."

The passengers glanced up from listening to the weapons dealer's lamenting aware that they were not alone. The steward had entered the module from the rear utility cabin that housed not only a small galley, lavatory, but also the subatomic engine that powered the levitation technology that kept the skimmer in motion. He stood studying the passengers the compartment contained.

He made, Sano thought, a fine figure of a male. A youth, but far from an adolescent, neatly trim in his uniform with the decals of service. His face was intense, somberly handsome, the mouth sensitive, the eyes dark, enigmatic. A male of controlled passions and, Sano suspected, a lonely one. Lonely with the isolation of travel, the distance that it carried.

The steward carried a tray of refreshments. Offering them, he said, "Arrival time at Oregana will be 15:30 local time."

Another sixty miles to go. Sano accepted a drink. He was too tense to eat, and Lamont did not help. He noticed the steward's name plate read *B. Daros*. He wondered the meaning of the '*B*'. Suddenly he wondered a lot about the handsome attendant. Their eyes met and both smiled appreciatively.

## CHAPTER THREE:

Captain Cross could not believe what he saw rising up from the pebbled path before the hurrying skimmer out the forward ports. His co-pilot seemed unable to resist stating the obvious. A line of boulders blocked their way, each stony pinnacle resembled a worn-down molar of some fossilized giant.

"Rockslide!" Breck Bezzerides exclaimed, slamming a palm down on the emergency braking control.

The skimmer skidded to a sudden stop at a skewed angle before a queerly positioned boulder obstacle barrier. The elevation engine groaned to a stop and the shuttle settled with ease on its four-point landing gear skids.

Unstrapping from his harness, Cross pulled himself up and out of his acceleration seat and headed for the exit. He was met in the exitportal by Sano Hille, wearing a puzzled expression. The captain quickly tabbed the fuselage's hatch egress control and the hot-baked desert air filled the airlock.

Stepping out to inspect the line of rock that blocked their way, Sano could not help himself and asked, "What's the trouble?"

From behind them a familiar voice answered, "There's no trouble. No trouble at all."

Turning the two recognized the begetter of the reply. While they focused their memory, two colleagues had entered the skimmer's exitportal airlock and could be heard issuing orders to the crew and passengers held within.

"Don't try it"

"Just get out, nice and easy like."

In single-file the skimmer's remaining complement stepped out of the shuttle and collected themselves loosely outside, all under the watchful eye of their assailants. Captain Cross locked eyes with the leader of the marauders.

"We've got nothing you want," he said.

"Fast as you can, thrown down your gun belts!" the leader snapped. "Thrown them down! Now!"

Compliantly, the crew and Hille males capitulated and unbuckled their holstered belts. Each thrown awkwardly to the sandy grit.

"Now, payroll!"

Bezzerides turned to retrieve the device from the command module, a secondary bandit followed him inside. Euphemia's eyes lit up with recognition of the octopod hominid.

"You! You were the rider this morning."

"Yes, Sinjorino…" the leader smiled, tipping his hat with his free-hand. "I was the one."

The co-pilot was taking too long to remove the data-blade from inside the cockpit. The third accomplice grew impatient. "Come on!" he ordered, waving his pistol at the assembled prisoners.

Bezzerides emerged from the airlock with the handled blade. His accompanying thief was close behind, weapon drawn. Unexpectedly, the co-pilot did not hand the data-containing cartridge to the marauder leader, but instead he pivoted, hit his escort square in the jaw, sending him sprawling, and then threw it at the leader's face. What followed was a blur of chaos from a gun discharging to the steward falling with a wound to his abdomen and the Hille boys tackling and wrestling the marauders to the ground.

Emilie screamed as a pistol was discharged by the leader in the air as he yelled, "That's enough!"

Then it was over. Everyone resumed their previous position, albeit covered in dust and dirt and bearing bruises on their faces. The marauder leader glared at the co-pilot. "No one needed to get hurt," he snarled, indicating the fallen youth. "All we wanted was the currency information. But you had to play it stupid. Well, you ain't gonna live now."

"Grouper!" the secondary male yelled out. "You kill one, you'll have to kill them all! You said so yourself. Let the desert do it. Its forty miles either way. Who's to know? Who's to say?"

The leader lowered his weapon and chuckled with a smile, "That's right. Who is to say?"

It didn't take long to empty the skimmer's cisterns, destroy the bus power and navigation controls, and rifle through the passenger's personal effects; destroying personal communication devices and absconding with valuables. Once the leader was certain that all the shuttle's water reserves were emptied, all means of powering the skimmer destroyed, communications were silenced, and no valuables were left behind, he said to his cohorts, "That's it. There's nothing else they can use. Off we go!"

Captain Cross rose from where he had crouched to examine the fallen steward, shouting, "Give us a chance! One canteen. The next shuttle won't be through here for three days."

The leader chuckled. "Wrong. Oh, friend, the shuttle won't be through at all. The rockslide I told you about this morning, there wasn't any. Only rockslide is the one we arranged, right here. So, don't be expecting anybody coming along this way. No one has for years. Have a nice walk."

With that, he lowered his weapon, straddled his purring hovercycle and joined his two comrades on the ridgeline. It did not take long for their diminishing figures to vanish over the brush horizon. It left a sudden void within those left behind. A feeling of utter abandonment, violation, and loneliness. Each wore their feelings differently on their expression, but collectively as a group they looked horribly despondent.

Worse of them all was the fallen steward who had taken the initial offensive fire during the scuffle. He lay quiet and pale on the earthen trail. His breath shallow and his face lax. Cross attended to him again, trying to ascertain his vitals by the most primitive means. The others could only watch helpless as the very life force of the boy seemed to dim with each fading breath.

## CHAPTER FOUR:

The wind whipped over the barren wasteland. Vast nothingness as far as the eye could see. Everything here seemed to combine against life.

One quarter of the planet's surface was covered in deserts. Many animals had made wonderful adaptations from splayed feet to biosensors that could detect heat and feathers that could transport water. Native creatures poked out of their burrows, scurried across the sand, and soared through the sky.

Under the burning primary sun, competition was extreme. Some of the rocks appeared to be roving on their own as tortoises fought for mating rights, as did the majestic blackbuck antelope with spiky antlers regally dueling. In far off distances, the local dromedary herds marched the horizon in single-file.

All revealed a landscape not as lifeless as it first appeared. Below the dust, the sand, the squashed rocks there were glitters of hope.

The semiarid air was moisture-deficient, evaporating water faster than received due to the rain-shadow effect. A track of land burned by the primary sun and shaped by the wind. The day's temperature was easily one hundred and twenty degrees.

Under the baked domed desert sky, the marooned group of travelers consolidated their situation. Euphemia and Emilie along with Sano made the injured steward as comfortable as possible while assessing and dressing his abdominal wound. They had made a makeshift mattress from coats and pillows from rolled up clothing. They used drippings from local spiny plants to clean the bleeding pulse-energy laceration. The youth was paper-white and too quiet.

All the while, Lamont nursed the last drops from his flask while on top of a boulder off to the side of the scene.

Captain Cross emerged from the exitportal of the skimmer along with Bezzerides, his face long and scornful. He took in the tableau grimly.

"The Sawtooth Mountains that way," he sighed, looking to his left. "Black Rock that way." He looked right. "What's it gonna be?"

Sano looked up from where he knelt beside the fallen steward and shook his head. "It's gonna be neither as far as I can see. In this heat with no water. He won't last a day."

Euphemia looked hopeful. "You know this country, Captain. Isn't there water anyplace?"

Cross frowned and shook his head. "I'm just a transport driver. I follow the roads."

"Once there were no roads," Lamont croaked out as he lowered his flask.

"What's that supposed to mean?" Bezzerides asked.

"Death always knocks twice." Lamont breathed heavily. "Perhaps…perhaps that's why I've been traveling through this country all these years. Realizing it till just now. He's won. Well when it's like before."

Rikard had reached his limit with patience. "Make sense, Lamont," he growled.

"We're what… eight…this time. Before there were thirty of them, lived as one. I was fortunate that time. I should have known."

"You mean you were out here like this before?" Rikard moved closer to the drunken seller. "And, lived? How?"

"None in his small wagon train and the water was low and there was supposed to be a passage through the mountains to a spring," Lamont slurred, pointing toward the distant elevation breaking the smooth horizon line. "But a scout guessed wrong and led them to the wrong mountain passage and there was no water, little spring. On the other side, there's another place… uh … a mining town called Salt Flats..."

"I've heard of it…"

"I made it there. Two of them. Got water and brought it back. Water is no good for twenty-seven dead people."

Euphemia spoke up, "If there was a spring, could you find the right way this time?"

"Sinjorino," Cross cut in politely. "Those mountains he's raving about are further away than we've come on the skimmer"

Lamont nodded, trying to stand from the boulder he sat upon. "Captain's right." He circled around to where the others had collected themselves around the fallen steward. "He'd never make it. Yeah. Unless … unless…"

"Unless what?!" Rikard insisted.

"Well, there was a place I remember was it was almost dried up," Lamont squinted toward the remote boundary. "But then it was the last place we got water …"

The inebriated seller trailed off discouraged. He turned to enter the skimmer, but Rikard caught him by his elbow and glared insistently at him. "Where was it, Lamont?"

Shrugging off the other's handhold, Lamont snapped, "I don't know! I guess back there somewhere." He turned and made his way into the shadowy confines of the airlock. "Excuse me," he said as he vanished inside the exitportal's opened hatchway.

Sano stood to stand beside his brother. "You know those males were no fools," he said into Rikard's ear. "They wouldn't make it out there either without any water."

Bezzerides was close enough to overhear and added, "Maybe if we follow them!"

Rikard cracked a smile of inspiration and turned toward where the hovercycles had motored from and said, "There's plenty of wake tracks."

Sano went inside the airlock, saying, "Just a minute." When he returned, he was carrying Lamont's carrying case. He promptly opened it and showed the others the display pistols. "Praise the Maker. The bandits overlooked something!" Over his shoulder, he shouted, "Lamont! Do you have ammunition charges for these pistols?!"

From the black square of the exitportal, the seller emerged and fiddled inside the opened case, producing a small box from a secret compartment in the lid. Captain Cross scooped up the box and opened it with zeal. He held up three small capsules, saying, "Not a lot of them to waste is there? I hope you don't need a lot of target practice."

"You'd never make it with or without those charge cartridges," Lamont said frankly, turning his flask over and trying to get the last drops of liquor from within it. "Excuse me," he said, dropping the empty flagon to the ground; it thumped hollowly. Then he rummaged through the case's false compartment again. He withdrew a fresh flask, presumed full.

Euphemia had seen enough self-medication for one day, she stood and approached the skimmer. "Sir Lamont!" she called out with intent.

The seller had seen that look before. "Now, you let me live my own life," he said forcefully. "What's left of it. My own way. I go away. You go follow those tracks, Sinjorino, give me something to do before you… I got something to do." He saluted her and took a long drink from the new flask.

"You drunk!" Emilie cursed under her breath loud enough for all to hear. "You no good rotten drunk."

Lamont smiled pleasantly and saluted her before reclining back into the recesses of the skimmer. Rikard softened his expression and simply said, "Leave him alone. He'll come when he's ready."

Bezzerides had slipped quietly back into the cockpit during the verbal exchange and stepped through the exitportal airlock hatch a few seconds after Lamont had entered. He was holding a handheld transmitter.

"Look what I found," he exclaimed. "They didn't take everything that might be useful!"

The co-pilot began fiddling with the compact radio, checking batteries, searching channels, turning it up and listening for voices in static. Emilie could have told him that the transmitter was useless by the carbon scoring that marred its silvery surface.

"Tower Control. I say again…" Bezzarides called out into the concealed microphone.

"Breck, we're out of range for that small device," Cross said. He swapped glances with Rikard Hille. They both had assessed what the bandits had left behind, scattered around the abandoned skimmer transport like rubbish.

"What do we do now?" Emilie sighed. "How the hell do we get out of here?"

"We don't," Cross said. "Not without every last one of us. We'll head north following the hoverbike tracks."

"What about Bert?" asked Bezzerides, indicating the steward.

"We can make a travois out of seat upholstery and deck carpet," Sano said.

Rikard assessed those with him, and he did his best not to get too pessimistic. The others sat around the fallen steward binding his wound, Emilie was shaking her head. Each looked as if they were surviving alone in this mess even if they sat next to one another. There was no unity here for them, no sense of being part of a team. Believing themselves doomed meant that they'd already given in to the marauders. Everyone remained silent, waiting for someone in authority to speak. Rikard Hille was that type of male.

He nodded, "Let's get started. Mother, will Emilie and you gather some wood for the travois supports? In this I am sure you can find enough to make a sturdy framework."

Both females nodded and set about the task.

Cross gestured to Sano, the young male still stood by the opened pistol case. "I'll take one," he said. "You and your brother take the other two. Don't forget the ammo charges, either."

The captain accepted the gun offered to him, as did Rikard. Sano loaded and tucked his pistol into his pants' waistline. From their faces, Cross could tell that both Hille males had not only held a gun before but had plenty of practice shooting one.

The others seemed boosted by the mobilization, ready to head out. They gathered themselves, trying to shake off the past. It was too immediate and too horrific to forget. Euphemia and

Emilie had found four long branches from a fallen mesquite tree and set about stripping off the dead bark and using it for binding the boughs together.

Cross grunted in satisfaction. His loathing burned deep, smothering fear and giving every sense an edge. He imagined the marauders down and dead by his hand.

It felt good to be taking action.

Once the makeshift travois was assembled, they moved out and headed north through the desert, following the tracks left behind by the bandits, searching for water. From now on, they would be looking to Rikard and Cross for words of advice before they headed off. Cross could think of many, but he wasn't sure any of them would save lives. Not in such a place, with such elements threatening them.

"We need to stay tight and move fast," he said, not looking back.

Time was ticking.

Counting the footsteps of those following. It was all of them, sans one.

## CHAPTER FIVE:

As the small group moved forward, sweaty and dirty, exhausted under the oppressive sun's heat, still scared, Bezzerides continued to monitor the radio. The static sang, fading in and out. There were no voices. It was if the desert was whispering about them in mocking tones; much as Lamont had eluded.

"Save it for when we get closer to the water source, Breck," the captain said. "If anyone else is out there, that's where they will be."

Bezzerides clicked off the transmitter and slung it across his back, dejected and defeated. They moved on in single file and remained alert, Rikard was in the lead and he paused frequently to look around and take stock. Sano and Cross held firm to the travois hauling an unconscious Daros. The desert seemed to know when something bad was about to happen in situations when attention wandered. Euphemia walked into Emilie when she came to a standstill. She barely seemed to notice the impact.

"What?" Euphemia asked, immediately on edge.

"Lamont," Emilie whispered.

Behind them, following their foot markings in the sand, the weapons dealer could be seen as a remote silhouette. At the pace they were keeping, it would not be long before he caught up with them.

Without further pause, the two females quickly made their way to join the males who had kept walking. Euphemia took notice of how weak Emilie seemed to become since they had left the skimmer. They had only covered a few miles and the female appeared unreasonably frail and tired. Old maternal instincts kicked in and Euphemia reached over and took the other female by the elbow, assisting her in continuing.

It was a good thing. In short time, Emilie stumbled and fell against Euphemia's support. The older female spread her stance wider and supported the younger as they both bent down and sat on a lichen covered outcrop of rock. Emilie grunted with exhaustion.

"Please," she pleaded. "I need to rest."

"Rikard!" Euphemia called out. "Sano!"

Lamont had made quick-time of matching the distance between the others and himself. He arrived just as Emilie had collapsed. Something clicked inside the old pessimist and he offered his flask to the fallen female.

"Here," he said. "It's better than nothing."

Emilie desperately reached out to accept the offer.

Cross arrived and jerked the seller's arm away. "Leave her alone," he ordered firmly. "It's the worst thing."

"I'm sorry," Emilie nodded. "I should have known. It's just that I am so thirsty."

"So much for the 'Greening Project'," Euphemia sniffed.

She was referring to the biggest water pipeline being built to tap into ancient underground water resources to help break the reign of dust and sand and make the desert region green. From her current perspective, she was doubtful of that vision becoming a reality. Her now-gone spouse had been a huge supporter of the venture. All around was an ocean of petrified wood, desiccated rock, and pulverized sand, nature's ultimate challenge. It truly was like being on an alien planet.

The travois had been lowered and Sano stopped to attend to a coughing Daros. He loosened the male's uniform tunic to give him some relief from the heat. The male's eyes were glazed and wandered. Sano had a sympathetic tinge and instantly felt protective of the wounded male.

Lamont shrugged free of Cross's grip and glared hotly back at the captain. Venting his anger, he pointed to the struggling steward. "He's gonna die," he barked. "Why not here. He's only holding us up."

Rikard called out to his brother.

Covering the steward with the blanket that wrapped him, Sano stood and moved toward his sibling. Rikard kept his eyes fixed on Lamont. Rage burned behind his stare.

"You take the lead," he said. "It's my turn on the travois."

With that, Rikard and Cross moved to take up the sled. Bezzerides joined Sano in the lead. Lamont lingered as Euphemia aided Emilie in standing.

"Are you alright?" the elder female asked.

Emilie nodded and accepted Euphemia's arm for support. Lamont nodded to them. Euphemia saw something different in him, but she wasn't sure what it was. He'd seen or experienced something out there in the desert. Something in his past he was reliving now. She'd ask him later.

Emilie did not protest when Lamont offered to also help her across the stony terrain as they continued. Euphemia suddenly saw a softer side to the cynical dealer. She couldn't help but smile, if even just a little.

They traveled without seeing a sign of life or a single bush or tree. Discouragement began to consume the troupe.

## CHAPTER SIX:

Bezzerides had wrapped a long piece of blue-dyed cotton fabric around his head and face in an amateurish imitation of a Tuareg. Just ahead of him, Sano froze. He pointed ahead at a clearing in the brush. It contained a wide sandy expanse, its surface relatively still and speckled with rocks and clumps of drought-resistant shrubs.

"What is it?" the co-pilot asked.

All around was a spectacular landscape of white limestone sculptures, created by the wind with sand as its tool. Arid and empty, scoured by the constant current of air. A draft had been gathering all afternoon, the air becoming oppressive, and the sky increasingly dull. In the earliest traces of dusk, ripples were breaking across the flattened gritsand and travelling across the large sun-blasted area. Liberated granules rode the undulations. The whisk of the wind could be heard. More sand began to move. Together the two elements formed spinning dustdevils that spun quickly across the barren plain.

"Sandstorm!" Sano identified. He turned and called out to the others. "Better take cover!"

The small band had happened on a rocky hillock with plenty of spaces to take refuge. As quickly as everyone could, they covered their mouths with cloths and hunkered down within the crevasses of the prominence. Sano made his way back to attend to the travois and Daros, using his own body to shield the steward as the bulk of the storm hit.

It began as a dance. The wind played games with the sand and the sand played along. Ephemeral flurries, a shape-shifting fabric of turbulence, scurrying grains.

A compelling and alluring show, but, at the same time, as the wind gathered, the air began to become oppressive and the brilliant sky took on a threatening dullness as the cargo of dust changed the spectrum. The ephemeral flurries became continuous sheets of sand hurtling across the desert surface, assailing everything in their path. The sun dimmed.

And then suddenly, seemingly out of nowhere, the streaming chaos turned into the full fury of a full-blown assault, threatening everything. It seemed as if the whole surface of the desert was rising in obedience to some upthrusting force from beneath.

Larger pebbles struck against shins, knees, thighs. The spray of dancing sand grains climbed their bodies till it struck their faces and went over their heads.

The sky was shut out, all but the nearest rocks faded from view, the world about filled with hurtling, pelting, stinging, biting legions of torment; as though some great monster of fabled size and unearthly power were puffing out hurtling blasts of sand upon the travelers' heads. The sound was that of a giant hand drawing rough fingers in regular rhythm across tightly stretched silk.

The eager sands swiftly gathered, piling up and up until there remained only a smoothly rounded heap. The storm drove the sand into everything one possessed. It filled clothes, food, baggage, instruments, everything. It searched out every weak spot in one's attire. One felt it, breathed it, ate it, drank it – and hated it. The finest particles even penetrated the pores of the skin, setting up a distressing irritation.

The earth was on the move. As miniature sand dunes migrated passed, and the hissing, spattering sound of the grains grew in volume, the burial process began. Piles of sand accumulated rapidly against the travelers' legs.

The storm raged through the night. Mercifully, the group fell into a calming sleep huddled together in stony clefts. When the noise ceased, it was morning. The dawn was miraculous. There was no sign of the storm other than the piles of sand marking buried rocks, but rather a crystalline clarity, a sense that the desert had been cleansed.

Colorful fowl flitted back and forth, digging at the ground and then flitting away with large winged insects in their beaks. Gnarled vertebrates leapt on and off exposed stones, adding to the animation. Exposed objects strewn all over the dune valley. The wind uncovering ever-new pieces and burying others.

"So, what's for breakfast?" quipped Lamont. "The sand grouse is known to nest in the center of the desert, fewer predators. Follow the flocks as they come to and from their nests in search of water and food for their brood. Perhaps y'all could scrounge up some eggs or an actual bird!"

The other males in the party looked at each other knowingly. Bezzerides gathered some stones in a circle while Sano and Cross went gathering firewood. Rikard would play hunter. The skies above were barren.

Euphemia and Emilie paid little attention to whatever eventually was roasting over the open fire. They were just grateful to still be alive.

Cross was surprisingly a good chef. He had made a primitive, but effective rotisserie from rejected kindling and now gingerly attended to the spit-roasting with seemingly practiced care. The rotation cooked the meat evenly in its own juices and allowed easy access for continuous basting.

Some of the items the captain had personally packed away before leaving the skimmer were survival camping supplies. Of which included plates and cutlery. He now used a fork and knife to slice off a piece of meat from the skewered carcass and place it on a plate.

Euphemia thankfully accepted the proffered meal while Emilie politely refused, looking nauseous. "Oh, no, please," she shook her head.

"It isn't that bad," Cross smiled. "Honest. Some even say it tastes like poultry."

"I think I feel…" Emilie whispered. "If you don't …"

"Please," the captain insisted.

Relenting, she took a small piece of meat and nibbled on it.

Satisfied, Cross stood and said, "I'll see if I can get some down Bert."

The travois had been laid down near the fire and the young male seemed groggily conscious. Sano was attending to the male when Cross arrived with the plate of cooked meat. Tenderly, the captain offered the suffering steward a small piece. "Here you go, Bert," he said.

Euphemia and Emilie watched hopeful. There was always hope.

"I remember when I was a little girl," Emilie shared. "My father used to say take what you can get and be thankful for it."

"Are you?" Euphemia asked. "Thankful?"

An awkward silence fell between the two females. It was more than just a lack of knowing what more to say to each other. One was keeping a secret and it was time she was called out on it.

"How far along are you?" asked Euphemia.

That was it. A truth finally out in the open. Emilie sighed almost from relief.

"Four months."

"I wish I could do or say something that would help you." Euphemia soothed. "Losing a spouse at a time when you need him most."

"There's nothing to say, Sinjorino Hille. My spouse was killed three years ago."

"Oh…"

Cross interrupted the tableau with harsh news. "He's bleeding again," he told the two females. He was referring to Daros.

Euphemia nodded and went to join her youngest child over by the travois.

Cross tenderly offered Emilie another bite of the plated meat. She kindly refused.

"No thank you. I've had mine."

"You go on. Take it. You gotta think about your other one," he knowingly smiled at her. His eyes held kindness, not judgement.

Humbled, Emilie accepted.

While she ate, Cross took noticed that Bizzerides and Rikard had joined the others around the camp's fire. They had ventured out to see what tracks remained after the storm. The expressions on their faces were not encouraging.

The captain approached the two as they dusted off their pants. "Well?" he asked.

"Nothing," Rikard said, disgusted. "No more tracks to follow."

"They blew away in the storm," Bezzerides added.

Cross nodded, accepting the inevitable. He held up the plate and offered the remaining meat to them. "Here. There's meat on it for you two."

While the males shared, Cross rejoined the travois for an update.

"He's burning up," Euphemia reported, saddened.

Sano looked over his shoulder at the self-medicating retailer. "What about you, Lamont. Any ideas?"

Lowering his flask, the male said, "I told you from the start…"

"You told us there was a water hole out here somewhere," Sano cut him off.

"That was ten years ago. Every day the desert changes. Sand where there weren't any. Rock that used to be a landmark gone. What do you want from me?" Lamont asked.

Turning he saw the weight of his words laying heavily on the others; especially Sano as he continued to cope with the injured steward. "He could have died back at the skimmer," he slurred, pointing at the travois' occupant. "You could do it here or take him out there and do it. What difference does it make to me…?"

Sano had heard enough. He stood bolt upright and confronted the drunk. "What's the matter with you?!" he insisted. "Are you afraid to try? Nobody's going to…"

"You leave me alone!" Lamont shouted back, standing clumsily. "You hear me?!"

The campsite went suddenly quiet. No one challenged the intoxicated male.

"Leave me alone!"

With that declaration, he stumbled away, behind an exposed boulder and collapsed behind it with a huff of forced air.

Cross took stock of the situation and the tension within the group. He stood and said in a calming force, "It would be better not to travel in the heat of the day. Let's get under cover and get some rest. We'll need it."

The others nodded and made their best arrangements for bedding, in shadows of every upright boulder and tree. Using the material they had brought along with them to make lean-to tents and sheltered under them.

Surprisingly, sleep came quickly and quietly to the travelers; except one. Emilie was plagued with unseen tormentors and howls from hidden sources. She tossed and turned in her attempts to flee from her harassers. She subconsciously called out for help.

Emilie woke to find Cross by her side. Her stressed features softened at the realization of her savior. "I was having a dream," she unnecessarily explained. "It comes back from time to time." She paused; the captain listened. "We had a ranch. Oh, nothing much, you know. Just …uh … just some cattle and a few crops, but it was home. I was happy until it stopped being a home."

"And…"

"For an Unling female," she explained, "her home is with her mate and mine was always there … working, planning … *'Someday,'* he'd say, *'Someday'*. Well, it did not happen, so no sense talking about it." She drew her shawl closer even though the heat of the morning was becoming felt more intensely.

"He must have cared an awful lot," Cross reflected.

"I don't remember what he looks like," admitted Emilie matter-of-factly. "I can hardly remember. It is said that sometimes happens. No offspring around to remind you, see him in their eyes, the way they look…" she trailed off, then looked at the captain squarely. She smirked. "Go ahead and say it. I know what you are thinking."

"Oh no. I wasn't thinking…"

"A female alone, she's gotta make out the best that she can. I'm not saying I did anything right, I guess I was …I was lost. Do you know what I mean?"

Cross silently nodded.

"Oh no you don't," Emilie sighed. "I knew a male. He seemed so different from the rest. He said he wanted to be joined in monastic vows with me. It was like being born all over again. Someone to share plans with again. A good life to look forward too. Then he left and I waited until I knew it was no use." She paused again. Then said, "I have a sister who lives in Oregana. Well, she used to live there. I have no other place to go to. I'm sure she's still there. I reached out to her, but…"

She stopped. There was a stirring behind them. From the travois. Daros was whispering deliriously about water being close by. Emilie looked at the captain with concern.

"Oh, he'll be just fine," Cross reassured. "Now get back to sleep. Sundown isn't for a few more hours."

What had to be said, had been said. There was no need to go on about what had happened and what she hoped would be waiting for her in the near future. Emilie smiled and then laid back down on her bedding, closing her eyes feeling somewhat relieved of a hidden burden. Cross waited till he saw the soft rise and fall of her chest before he returned to his sleeper and happily closed his eyes.

The wandering whispers of Daros went unheard by the sleeping complement. They did not hear his ravings for water, nor did they take notice that his delirium had him crawling desperately from his sled out over the campsite and into the burning desert in a futile quest. A new set of tracks was made that morning, those of a creeping body into the monotonous wasteland.

## CHAPTER SEVEN:

A scouting party of Sano, Rikard, and Bezzerides had found him. A still, prone form under desert scrub. Bert Daros was dead due to exposure. His head lay at an odd angle, his handsome face held a pleasant expression. Perhaps he had found peace at last.

The rest of the party joined in making a stone mound grave. Remorsefully, they gathered in a loose circle around it to pay their last respects. Each face held a different version of the same emotion. Sano especially took it hard; he was beginning to have ties to the male. Feelings he had not felt for another in a long, long time.

Cross knew that the time was upon them to get moving, they were losing precious time. The sun was low on the horizon and the day was quickly burning off into a noticeable chill. He signaled to the others that they needed to move on.

Reverently, the travelers gathered their meager belongings and followed Cross onward, leaving the abandoned travois behind.

The small party was down one, but that didn't make the traveling any easier. By morning's twilight, Emilie had gone about as far as she could. Cross took noticed and helped her take a seat on a smooth boulder.

"Here," he instructed. "You rest."

"No. I am fine."

"We all could do with a rest," Euphemia said, sitting down on the rock beside Emilie.

The males split up and leaned against various outcroppings. Ever vigilant, Rikard turned to the sobering dealer and asked, "Lamont, what do you think? We headed in right direction?"

"I think so. If I didn't think so, I would have told you." He stared out into the distance. Looking intently at the configuration of stones, boulders, and horizon. "Everything looks the same…" he muttered. The landscape was dull, tedious, and repetitious; lacking in variety. Not one thing looked familiar. Not one …then he saw it. A projecting rock feature sticking out and up and at a familiar angle, forming a known shape. "There! Why didn't I see it before?!"

"What?" insisted the others in unison.

Lamont pointed glibly at a remote rock feature. "There! Finger Rock. Why didn't I make it out before? The wagon train… we were coming from the southeast, not this way. You see, this way it looks different. That's why I didn't see it, why I didn't make it out! That's the water hole!"

He took off like a child. Suddenly he was a sober adult with a mission. The others quickly found energy they thought they had lost and ran with him, over rough terrain, around boulders, and down into a shallow depression with the pointy rock cantilevered above.

Encircling a moist patch of earth was a copse of ocotillo. Known to thrive in hot and dry climates and did exceptionally well in low water environments. The scene looked promising. Emilie was overcome with joy and dashed to take a drink from the pool.

"Stop!" shouted Lamont. He intercepted her, throwing her bodily from the reflecting water. It was muddy and had an odd coloring and smell. "It's not fit!"

The others gathered and saw and smelled it too. Foul water. Even the surrounding ocotillo looked brown and partially withered. Soiled by the earth.

Lamont chuckled, raising his flask. "Now maybe all of you will join me in a drink." He offered it with an outstretch arm. "Huh? Now maybe you will have one on me. Come on. Drink up. Enjoy yourselves. It's all you got. Nothing else. No?"

The others just stared in complete despair. In frustration, Lamont tilted his head back with the flask secured in the lock of his cracked lips and drank down the last of the fiery liquid. Emptied, he threw the drained flask in the goopy water and staggered over to sit on a dusty boulder.

One by one the others reclined in various positions along the ring of ocotillo trees. Sanos leaned forward and removed the muck covered flask and stared at it. His eyes sparkled.

An idea was forming. He looked at his fellow companions to see if they were thinking the same as him. They just stared back blankly. He removed a handkerchief from his pants back pocket and covered the nozzle of the flask with it. He then placed the flask back into the dirty water, bubbles fizzled around the penetration point.

Air was exchanged for liquid. When the gurgling stopped, Sano pulled the bottle out and removed the muddy handkerchief.

Inside the flask clear liquid could be see reflecting the morning light. Cautiously, Sano placed the flask opening to his lips and tilted it. Cool, filtered water quenched his parched mouth and throat, all the way to his shrunken stomach. It tasted better than nectar. There was just a hint of alcohol.

This action had everyone's attention. Sitting upright they all observed Sano's reaction to drinking from the muddy flask. When they saw him smiling, they all exhaled.

Sano offered Emilie the container. "Just a sip," he advised.

She eagerly drank and then passed the bottle on to Euphemia, who did the same and gave it to Rikard. The flagon was given to everyone in the party from Rikard to Bezzerides to Cross to Lamont, then back again to Sano. It was a well needed victory.

The impromptu canteen was refilled four times before the fatal news that the well had gone dry came. "That's the last of it," Sano huffed. "We got all that was left."

The travelers took it in stride. Rikard started planning.

"Lamont," he said. "When we get to those mountains, which way do we start up?"

The male just shrugged.

"Come on, Lamont. You found this place. What was it you said? Ten years ago, that scout that was leading your wagon train, he made a mistake."

"That's right. He made a jump into the wrong pass. No spring. No water. All those people died."

"Except you."

"Me and two others."

"You made it out. Found the right pass. Found the spring. Made it across the salt flats. Got help. Only when you got back, it was too late."

"You got that all wrong," Lamont corrected. "We never found that spring."

"You mean you were able to get across that desert, in all that heat with no water?" Rikard was in disbelief. "How? You must have had water."

"No, we did not. Where would we get water? There's nothing between this place and Salt Flats of that spring…"

"Which you did not find." Rikard cocked his eyebrow quizzically, saying, "But you found Finger Rock."

"What are you saying?

"You have a strange hatred for this desert, Sir Lamont," Rikard said calculatingly. "That bottle that you've hidden behind all these years. Bad memories? Nightmares?"

"You watch what you say to me," Lamont warned. "You hear?"

Rikard rose up from his crouched position. "Who are you Sir Lamont?" his tone held a challenge. "A pistol purveyor?"

"I suppose so."

"A drunk, that's obvious."

Lamont stood, too. "Where do you get off talking to me like that?!" he shouted.

"Ten years ago, that was something different. Wasn't it, Sir Lamont?!" Rikard allowed his rage to surface. His face pinched into a countenance of utter hatred. "You were something different. You were the one that made that mistake and led those people up into the mountains to die…"

"No…"

"You were the one!" Rikard grabbed the other by his soiled collar. He brought his face with inches of the other. Their hot breaths intermixed. "You were the guide for that wagon train!"

Lamont's body went limp and Rikard released him, to fall back onto the rock that he had just moments ago been seated upon. The tension that had been building within the area popped like an invisible bubble. The truth was out. Subconscious whispers within each traveler's mind went silent. Their intuitions had been right. Now they all knew.

Try as he might, Lamont could not speak to the shocked and judging faces that glared at him. He opened his mouth to respond, but no words formed. He had been caught in his lies. There was nothing more to be said. Except more truth.

"All right!" he said. "I was that scout. I was that scout!" Pent up emotions over-boiled and he sobbed openly. "Those people I was leading were so in a hurry to get to Oregana. I pleaded with them. I said to go slow. Go round about. Along the mountains, there's plenty of water there. They wouldn't listen to me. No. Through here as fastest. They were paying me. If I didn't do it, they would have hired someone else."

He calmed down and went on. "I got them this far. There wasn't any more water here than what we found here just now. I didn't know those hills. I'd heard of a pass and a spring. I had to get them out of here. I had to guess. It's their only chance. Well, I guessed wrong and when we got there, there was no spring. No water." He seemed to drift off into some reminiscent trail of thought, adding, "When we took their water, I figured if I could make it to Salt Flats, I could bring back plenty of water. I figured…"

"What did you say?" Sano cut him off.

"You took *their* water?!" Euphemia growled.

"Those two other males, they forced me to with a gun," Lamont tried to explain, to appeal to them. "You see, I was their guide. I was their scout, they needed me, and they threatened to kill me if I didn't. I told them that there was only one canteen of water in that whole wagon train. Half, I said, just leave them half. They took the whole thing. Took all of it and left them there to die.

"That was ten year ago. I never talked about it. Never mentioned it before … want to know why?" he met their gazes equally. "Look at you. Look at your faces. That's why! I should have let those males kill me."

Sano sighed and stood. "Fine, Lamont. You were wrong once," he said. 'Do you think you can get it right this time?"

"No. Nobody is gonna make me guess wrong again."

"We're not making you," Euphemia called out desperately. "We're asking you! Try! Just try!" She beat her clenched fists into the dirt. Her eyes raged with distress.

Lamont noticed the change in the others' expressions. Collectively, they all had softened, seemed to appeal to him now. They were at their last option. They were choosing him. He slumped his shoulders and sighed, shaking his head at their stupidity.

## CHAPTER EIGHT:

Even though the landscape remained arid, there were beginning to be subtle changes in elevation and plant life, even the occasional wildlife. Lamont led the party up and out of the water hole depression, down into a rocky gorge, and then up into the beginnings of hillier country. He preferred moving during the day, seeing where he was going instead of hoping for the light of the moon to reveal what lay underfoot and ahead.

The only relief came from a desiccating breeze. It ruffled their dirty hairs and the fabric of their sweat-sodden clothing. But still no water revealed itself. It was apparent something was wrong.

Lamont stopped still.

"What's the matter?" Rikard asked.

"I did it again! I made the same mistake again!" the guide raged. "The wrong pass!" He stared at the ridgeline ahead of them and huffed. "Twenty-seven people are buried up there."

"We're never going to make it any other way." Rikard looked as drained as he sounded. "It's too late. It'll be dark soon. We keep going on when it's cooler. Maybe we'll get over."

"Nothing's on the other side," Lamont told him. "Salt Flats is an easy twenty more miles."

"There's nothing here," Euphemia said, her voice once again husky with thirst.

Lamont simply nodded and continued to lead them on.

By the time they reached the height of the mountains, it was dark, and they were spent. Euphemia did not wait to be told, she just laid down on the nearest soft spot of earth. Cross was with Emilie and they followed suit.

"Lamont," Rikard coughed. "How far now?"

"In about half a mile, maybe we'll be over then," he said, resting against the base of a large boulder sheltering a clump of lichen ferns.

"And, after that," Euphemia ventured. "Twenty more?"

"Rest, Mother," Sano comforted. "Just rest."

A fire was built and just in time. Night fell suddenly and the temperature dropped to almost freezing due to the extremely low humidity.

Unlike in more temperate regions where the humidity in the atmosphere stores the warmth of the day, soothing out the difference between day and night. In this desert, the warmth was gone as soon as the primary sun set, but the clear air opened the views into the sky.

The moons seemed closer than anywhere else on Para. A viridian ban of twilight encircled the jagged mountain tops like a cast-off ribbon as the two secondary system stars weakly manipulated circadian rhythms from their far-off distances.

Emilie and Cross seemed not to care about what Lamont had to say. They were just glad to be alive, and together. "It's cooler," she said.

"Yeah. It's that way most places when night comes. Like my place, after sundown. Crickets kicking up a song, frogs down by the stream croaking away, big old trees sighing in the breeze. Doesn't that sound nice?"

"Everybody's got to have a place to look back on to call home." Emilie seemed to purr, "It's a need."

"I do." Cross drew closer to her, adding, "I'd like you to think about my place."

Emilie was caught off-guard, almost blushed. "Well, thank you, Captain…"

"Charlie, please."

"Thank you very much, Charlie. I'd like to do that. Thank you." She settled against a rock, smiling – for the first time in too long of a time.

The two newly acquainted gazed high above into the night sky to see the bright pinpoint-light of stars and fellow planets. Moons hung low in the nocturnal dome. Each atmosphere of the moons was a very scant presence of gases surrounding each satellite.

For most practical purposes, each was considered to be surrounded by vacuum. Their phases waned, waxed, and even sometimes could not be seen during their phases. That was until they were settled first by miners, then urban planners that allowed pressurized development sprawl to grow across their surfaces like a living acne.

Tonight was the beginning portion of the moons' phases, happening when the moons were located between the primary sun and Para. Typically, these 'new moons' could not be seen since their dark sides faced Para. Such placing could create solar eclipses where each moon blocked the primary sun's rays and created shadows on parts of Para.

But the moons were not absent of life. Fanning out from slim crescent terminator lines, blotches of phantom light created by urban areas on Para's satellites gave a whole new meaning to the phrase 'night lights'. Like far off bizarre chandeliers seen from below the designs hung pressed hauntingly overhead. The nighttime views showed how patterns of corporeal settlements had changed over time on the moons.

"There is Lunula Base," Captain Cross pointed to a specific set of rings spanning out in a concentric motif. "And, Krunt Zazra," he identified another illuminated swatch. "S'relar City…"

"Funny how it was when I was back on Un, how easy it was to identify them back at school," Emilie reminisced. "We used to just sit there in class and rattle them off."

"Do you wanna go home, Emilie?"

"I never did like school."

The tenebrous drama of nyctophilic lives unfolded blindly around the campers' awareness as they sat ringed around the small fire circle of stone. Secrets of the unknown filled the noise envelope. An impromptu surround sound concert of serenading nocturnal insects rose into and out of crescendo. The occasional warning wail of fleeing ungulates pursued by a stalking felid punctured the arthropod sonnets as a kind of musical declamation. As if mythology had come to life. Warrior-maidens riding through the air on their steeds, calling for heroes killed in battle to Valhalla, bringing them to the home of the gods, to form a garrison of defense.

Emilie grinned as she thought of the connection, laughing under her breath.

"What?" asked Cross, noticing her smile.

"Just the night sounds," she explained, sheepishly. "To me, it sounds like what the female messengers of the god Odin, riding into battle on their flying horses and taking the souls of dead soldiers to Valhalla would be. Silly, yes?"

"Silly, no," Cross smiled back. "How very cultured of you."

Emilie just nodded and shyly tilted her head, lowering her gaze.

"I wonder if they up there are looking down on us down here," mused Cross, pointing to the lunar tapestry of pin-spot patterns stitched together with a free hand.

"If they are," Emilie smiled, gently edging her way closer into the bend in the captain's elbow now over her shoulder, "I hope they are with someone has gentle and kind as I am."

Euphemia felt better now that she had rested. She saw the others were already recuperating from the long trek. "I think it's time we went on," she said.

No one seemed to object, so she stood and dusted herself off. The others followed, looking at what mountain they had yet to conquer. That's when Sano noticed a flickering amongst the contours.

"That looks like a fire up there," he announced.

"Could be Amerinds," Lamont cautioned.

"Maybe they are friendly."

"If not, you better act as if you have a full charge in that pistol you are carrying," Lamont warned.

Rikard went to stand beside his sibling, and said over his shoulder, "Captain, you stay here with the females."

"Lamont, we may need you, come on," Sano ordered, moving forward.

Bezzerides took up the rear guard, following Lamont and Rikard and Sano into the hilly night. Quick as they could, the foursome made their way through the desert highland and soon found themselves in a small grotto where a light seemed centered and flickered hauntingly.

Parked just outside the ring of light the fire cast were hovercycles. All too familiar. Their ignition starters were missing. Self-preservation had the males hunker down and approach with even more caution, pistols draw and ready. And sure enough, camped out by the campfire were the bandits that had stranded them. Sound asleep by the aid of whiskey, emptied bottles were cast aside around the site.

"Looks like they are moving slow," Rikard whispered. "Enjoying themselves."

"Span out," Sano said. "Try to get the drop on them."

"Lamont," Rikard said. "You stay here."

Slowly, deliberately, the Hille males and Bezzerides moved to create a crossfire. When in place, Rikard picked up a rock and threw it into the fire. The pyroclastic effect was enough to wake at least one of the marauders.

"Wake up!" he shouted to his cohorts.

It was the leader and he turned and found himself straight in Sano's sights.

"Drop it!"

The first shot from the bandit octopod leader was his last. It missed and Sano's return retort hit square in the target's chest. He fell without purpose, landing at a strange, broken angle with appendages askew. The bleeding body let out a ragged sigh and then went still.

Rikard dived in and fired at the second marauder to awake before he could get his weapon unholstered. The third was off at a run beyond the light of the fire, disappearing into the night like the thief that he was. Rikard's singing energy bolts chasing futilely after him.

Secure that the third larcenist was gone, Rikard and Sano and Bezzerides moved fully into the encampment. The downed two muggers were truly dead.

"He won't be heading for Salt Flats," Sano sniffed, referring to the escapee. "And, like the male said, there won't be anybody coming by."

Bezzerides smiled, and said, "I'll go get the others."

Lamont had not been idle during the altercation. He sought out a safe distance from the action. In doing so, he inadvertently stepped on softened earth that had a 'squish' to it when pressure was placed on it. It felt spongy. Looking down and around, he could not believe what he saw. It had to be a mirage.

Water. A shining pool of fresh, drinkable water.

Laughter filled the air. A cackle. It was a queer noise to reverberate around the encircling mountainsides. It almost sounded ethereal. Tracking the source, the two armed males found Lamont on his hands and knees, sobbing.

"What…" Rikard began, but then suddenly stopped.

Sanos was already joining Lamont by the pool and scooping up handfuls of water into his eager, wanting mouth. Rikard abandoned his inhibitions and knelt in kind.

Their nightmare was over.

Somewhere in the background, a thunderclap applauded their survival. The ambient light dimmed, and a cloudburst began to shower the land with a well-needed drink. The small group could not help but dance in celebration.

## CHAPTER NINE:

Daybreak chased shadows away. The desert put on a glittering fast-moving and colorful show.

Five lakes had formed in what was a gigantic caldera, an ancient collapsed volcano had blossomed into an oasis. Seeds that had been dormant for many years germinated, flowered, and set new seeds. The blooms attracted insects which in turn attracted insect-eaters and the fruit-eaters. In the heady atmosphere of growth and abundance everything big and small thrived.

Birds flocked in and with them predators of both air and land. The life cycle of the plants and animals accelerated by the harsh conditions so was the switch between wet and dry.

Once the clouds were gone, the primary sun soon reestablished its dominance. The oasis was just as susceptible to desert heat as the dusty plains that surrounded it. Gallons of water lost to evaporation.

Surrounded by thousands of miles of bare rock and dust, the five lakes pop-up oasis appeared to have literally dropped out of the ethereal pink sky.

It was a miracle. Euphemia wouldn't hear of any other explanation. She sat beside Emilie filling canteens along the pool's bank. The hidden glade was beautiful. The pond rested in a shallow surrounded by fruit-bearing trees.

"Follow the law of the desert," Euphemia spoke up enthusiastically. "Quick feast and then a long famine."

The water tasted like nectar, crisp and cool despite the warmth of the air. The fruits were darkly yellow beneath a purple rind, seedless, the juice thick and of the flavor of honey. The porous earth was drying up. The unforgiving desert environs returning.

"You know, Sinjorino Hille," Emilie said, "you never did say why you were traveling out here."

"Oh, well, Rikard had some legal business in Oregana with a business investor from Ĉielo Station," the elder female explained. "And, Sano wanted to look at a new strain of cattle being bred there, I have some friends there and... I don't know... I guess you could say I was on a holiday."

Rikard approached the two females as they capped the canteens.

"We'd better be going," he said. "We found the ignition starters."

There was no need to say where, the two females knew. On one of the corpses no doubt. Out of respect, they had been buried, like Daros had been.

Lamont loaded up one of the hovercycles with supplies, saying, "You know, I don't know how I could have missed it before."

"What month did you come by here, Lamont?" asked Rikard.

The male paused, thinking, remembering. "Hmmm. In the middle of Tayad."

"This is the end of Lunius," said Sano. "Summer's just really starting to boil."

"By Tayad, every spring in these hills will be dry," Rikard told him. "You didn't make a mistake Lamont, and you did not guess wrong. You brought those people to the right place."

"You gotta figure nature, Sir Lamont," Cross piped in. "Whether it comes natural like...like that desert dirt or hominid, like us. Either way it can bust up a person pretty bad or give him a new life."

With that, he reached down and drew Emilie into his embrace. She was hesitant and Euphemia gave her a bit of advice.

"Don't question it," she said, sweetly. "This time."

Emilie smiled back at Sinjorino Hille and accepted the captain's escort to one of the hovercycles. She straddled back of him as he took his place before the steering handlebars.

Rikard and Bezzerides with Lamont took the second cycle, while Euphemia rode as Sano's passenger. Supplies renewed and stolen equipment and data blade recovered, navigating to Oregana would be just as easy as when in the skimmer.

Collecting into a single-minded group, Captain Cross led the rest of the way from the Salt Flat Mountains eastward toward Oregana without a hitch. The rising sun soon setting to their backs in true heroic fashion.

# Llel

## Nepantlera

**CHAPTER ONE:**

The planet Llel was third from its star system's red primary sun. It was a telluric planet composed primarily of silicate rocks. A place where all manner of unusual life forms, from quasi-dinosaurs to intelligent carnivorous plants were native.

Secluded from galactic turmoil by its location in a little-visited sector of space, Llel was an astrophysical rarity. Surrounded by several moons, the planet contained a band of habitable atmosphere among its endless clouds.

In this stratum of life, enterprising prospectors had established floating trade complexes devoted to being centers for exploration, interstellar trade, and political maneuvering. The most well-known of these ventures was the opulent Coventry, floating in the planet's upper atmosphere.

Suspended high among the pastel clouds of Llel was a floating metropolis of sophisticated beauty and political freedom. A remarkable architectural feat of civil engineering. Often, the rotund city was mistaken for a Fata Morgana by those viewing it from below, a vapory mirage.

The city floated 8.848 kilometers above the surface of the planet. It contained a large and famous luxury resort district on its upper levels, complete with hotels and casinos. It consisted of 192 levels, in addition to level zero, a top-side surface-level plaza concourse. Some of the nearby floating settlements, like

Nimbus, and industrial platforms were also considered part of the city. The last official census placed Coventry's population at 1,427,000. As planetary total population was estimated at 4 million, the city was by far the dominant settlement on Llel.

Antigravity engines and tractor beam generators kept the city afloat and in position.

Coventry existed not only as a colony, but also as a sanctuary for those trying to escape the turmoil gripping other outlying worlds. Though profitable, Coventry was small enough not to be noticed by larger authorities such as the Colonial Consortium. It prospered under the capable stewardship of Baroness-Administrator Addilyn Danica.

Inhabited mainly by native Llelans, a spacefaring, bipedal ornithodiran species, the floating citadel demonstrated their mastery of advanced technology, resembling an aviary more than a typical metropolis with non-avianoid race residents. Unique corporeal beings having three pairs of limbs: legs, arms, and wings; their feathered wings allowed them to fly as well as hover.

Once a war-mongering race, priding themselves in the ability to rapidly breed vast armies. In the modern era, a united people dedicated to peace; a great and civilized nation. The general population upright bodies uniformly a snowy white layer plumage with black flight feathers visible only when their wings were spread. On males, a small patch of ornamental feathers on the chest became yellow in spring; both genders' bills and legs a yellow-orange. Immature cockerels mostly white as well, but the head, neck, and back variably dusky.

In native Llelese, the word Nepantla defined an in-between state, that uncertain terrain one crossed when moving from one place to another, when changing from one class, race, or sexual position to another, when traveling from the present identity into a new. A concept used in Llelan anthropology, social commentary, criticism, literature and art. Such was the time for many of its adolescent citizens.

## CHAPTER TWO:

The dresses took a year to sew, and the pullets spent a year learning how to wear them: how to glide, how to float their arms out so they never touch the skirts, how to hold their heads under the weight of the coiffure, how to fold their wings a daintily as possible. The dresses weighed so much—up to one hundred pounds—that they hurt the pullets that wore them.

Bruises at the shoulders and hips where the dress bones pulled down on pullet bones, fine downy torso feathers crushed. The dresses, like the gestures, were passed down from mother to daughter.

Each pullet needed five dressers, who first laced her into her corset, then affixed the "cage" of the hoop skirt to her waist, sneaking a pillow between the cage and her body so her skin wasn't rubbed raw. Then came petticoats, and the dress on top.

The dressing occurred over a tarp with a hole cut into its center, and once everything was in place, the attending matrons picked up each pullet and the tarp together and walked her to the stage so that the dress never touched the ground. If it was raining, they wrapped her in plastic too.

When she walked her presentation gait, she took the smallest steps possible, so she appeared to be borne along on a current of air. Large steps made the giant hooped skirt slap back and forth like a ringing bell.

A stately, exhibitive pace was key. Her arms remained at attention, hovering lightly above the hips of the dress, elbows soft, wrists tilted, hands in a poised claw. Wings held so tightly against the back as if to appear as part of the bodice. These subtle positions were a staple of the contemporary pageant:

the ritual gestures, all bodies made to form the same shapes—back rod-straight in the corset, head erect, smile mannered.

For the pullets, the hardest task was the curtsy, learning to sink to the floor gracefully and then rise again as if the momentum on their hips were only a trick of light. They taught each young female to do it in a little group in the salon, all of them laughing while wrapping around ruqun, platform sandals elevating their toeclaws, and beak liner already done.

"You go slowly onto one knee", a matron explained.

"Then, while remaining motionless from the waist up, tuck the other knee underneath for extra support," another added.

"'Slowly, sit down and back on your heels and bow magisterially over your imaginary skirts, keeping your chins up, up, up until the last moment, don't forget your uropygium feathers as well, when you finally accede to the skirt, turning the right cheek," a third demonstrated. "And no matter what you do, do not ruffle your plumage!"

It looked in the final phase like the pullets were cocking one ear to the dress, listening for what was underneath. The youths could not help but giggle at the sight.

"Why?" one pullet asked. "Why is this the bow?"

The matrons shrugged. "It's always been this way. That's how our matrons taught it to us." After a pause, they chanted in unison, "Peace be maintained."

The youthful females frowned, nodded and repeated the pledge.

## CHAPTER THREE:

There were many debutante balls within Coventry, and several pageants featured historical costumes, but the Society of Coventry Pageant and Ball in Central Hub was the most opulently patriotic among them.

In the late 40s, a few settlers from the East were sent to staff a new military base in the southwest Coventry Territories, a region that had recently been ceded to Coventry after the Heretic War. They found themselves in a place that was tenuously and unenthusiastically Coven. Hence the construction of the cloud city, christened with the same name as the territory battlefield.

Feeling perhaps a little forlorn at being so starkly in the minority, new arrivals established a local chapter of the lamentably named Improved Order Of The Discipled (IOOTD). Members of the order dressed as "Disciples," called their officers "Father," and began their meetings, or "congregations," by banging a hand-held hoop instead of a gavel.

The Improved Order Of The Discipled fashioned itself as a torchbearer for colonial-era Coventry patriotism, and its young Territory chapter was eager to enshrine that culture down at the border. So, it formed the Coventry's Celebration Association (CCA).

For the inaugural celebration, in '97, they 'laid siege' to the Old Territory City Hall, pretending to be a warring native heretic tribe conquering the city. The optics here must have been confusing, as the order was made up of immigrants, while most of the city's residents were indigenous. A young female was appointed to play a heretic, and after brokering peace between the tribe and the city, she received the keys to the Territory in appreciation of her efforts.

The siege was done away with long ago, but every First Season since '98, the CCA has thrown a massive festival—Coventry's largest, most elaborate party for its first reformation. Lately, the festival included a Prayer Jam for Salvation, a Founding Fathers' 5K Fun Fly, a Levin Bread Festival, a Holy Mother Pageant and Ball, an ecclesiastical-sponsored citywide parade, and so on.

The prestige event of the season was the pageant and debutante ball hosted by the Society of Coventry Pageant and Ball, which was started by CCA wives in '40 with the aim of adding glitz to the festival. Their daughters dressed up in what was creatively imagined to be Pre-Enlightenment-like attire (in fact, the dresses were not much like what Conservatives would have worn), playacting historical figures who might have been known at that time. Each year, one adult Society member was chosen to play First Mother herself, and a man from the WCCA is asked to play First Father.

The CCA was started by members of The Territory's mostly-indigenous upper class, but in the almost one hundred years since the association's founding, the city had become almost entirely mixed-ethnicity: on the '10 census, 96 percent of the population identified as Immigrated.

Through intermarriage, the upper class of The Territory had come to include not only the Indigenous but also the Immigrated. Today the pullets were mostly Immigrate Coventryans. Many of them descend from the original CCA families, but just as many were descended from the people who were categorically oppressed—and, in several instances, massacred—by a Coventry colonialist expansion set in motion by the Founding Fathers they dressed up to honor.

## CHAPTER FOUR:

In Nahuatl, there was a word for in-betweenness: *nepantla*. The Immigrants started using the word in the new century when they were being colonized. *Nepantla* meant "in the middle," which was what they were: between a past they wrote themselves and the future that would be written by their conquerors, in the middle of the river between who they had been and who they were allowed to be now.

Theorists have used the word shattered to describe the liminal existence of *nepantleras*, indicating both brokenness and the possibility of making something radically new. The word had also been used to describe the borderlands experience, the mixed-race experience, the experience of anyone who lived both in and outside their world of origin. *Nepantleras* were "threshold people."

A threshold crossed with the offering up of the most beautiful pullets to the Society Fathers. Their offspring would continue the propagation of doctrine and the security of The Coventry for generations yet to come.

Anxiously, each young pullet paraded themselves before their future husbands with the hope of success in as much of their eyes as in their frozen facial expressions. Consummation would be their reward for their year's-long practice and study.

A successful pregnancy their highest honor for existence. A purpose for being met. Anything less would not only be a personal disgrace, but also to their entire lineage.

The courtship between a Nepantleras pair lasted much longer than the actual act of copulation. Courtship behavior included several stages, from initially claiming territory to actually wooing a prospective mate's parents' approval with visual and auditory displays such as stunning plumage, spectacular flights, intricate songs, and elaborate dances. The courtship period was when a male cockerel Llelian showed off his health and strength to convince a female's parents that he was her best possible mate and would help her create the strongest, healthiest chicks with the best chance to survive.

Singing was one of the first steps in meeting approval. The song's intricacy or the variety of different songs one male Llelian could produce helped advertise its maturity and intelligence, highly desirable characteristics for a healthy mate. Singing also defined the boundaries of territory, warning off weaker competition. Afterward, during the mating ceremony, the newly-paired then created a duet as part of their bonding ritual from his wooing songs.

Flamboyant plumage colors and elaborate displays of prominent feathers, skin sacs, and body shape showed off the strength and health, advertising his suitability as a mate. Llelian cockerels were known for their stunning display with extensive, colorful fan tails. Others used subtle changes in posture to show off their plumage to the best effect, such as raising a crest, hunching their shoulders, or flaring their wings.

Physical movements, from daring dives to intricate sequences including wing flaps, head dips, bill rubbing, or different steps were part of the courtship ritual. The male alone danced for his female's matron while she observes his actions, after which both partners would interact with one another. Mistakes in the dance showed inexperience, weakness, or hesitancy and would not likely lead to successful mating.

Close contact between male and female birds was also part of the courtship rituals to help diffuse their normal spatial boundaries and aggression. The Llelian prospective pair lightly preened one another, sat with their bodies touching, or otherwise leaned on one another to show that they were not intending to harm their partner.

Offering food was another common part of courtship. A Llelian cockerel brought a morsel to the female, demonstrating that he was able not only to provide food but also that he could share it and provide for her while she incubated eggs or tended chicks. Bringing food and leaving it nearby for her to eat or he placed a seed or insect directly in her mouth just as he might be expected to do when helping feed hungry nestlings. Each familial congregation had their own set expectation.

Lastly, to be considered as a mate a suitor would show off their architectural skills. Constructing nests before the female arrived as a way to claim territory and show the suitable nesting areas they defend. Also decorating the nest with pebbles, moss, flowers, or even litter to make it more eye-catching. The female's parents may then choose the nest they prefer.

So many hoops to jump through, but in the end when approval was met by each rockery's Council of Matrons, the males were individually given an acceptance number and told to wait for the ceremonial matching to see the outcome of all his efforts. That day had come, this day.

Dressed in traditional silk asymmetric Sherwani in a rich navy blue and off-white Jodhpur pants, the male suitors waited impatiently for the drawing of numbers in the main courtship hall. Each males' plumage preened and washed, enhanced by their attire's buttons and silk work crafted long coat-like garment with half-collar neck and full sleeves which only served to highlight each male's unique hue of feathering. Wings folded tightly against their jackets, while tail feathers splayed and tucked at random, showing anxiousness.

Elaborate pastries were not of course a part of the daily diet. The most elegant of them were made for couplings. A union was a very important occasion indeed, for as was true with most isolated peoples, the respect for females was unusually high here, and old customs were clung to with deep devotion born of mistrust of change. So around a coupling ceremony most of all clung the old, familiar ways, centuries old.

Music was part of tradition. Celebrators were the heart and life of the honoring, dancing round and round, with loose-linked arms. They shuffled around and back. It gave great pleasure to those who took part.

Guests stopped by for a look at the union gifts, laid out before the roosting chambers' closed doorways. Many of the females wore simplistic outfits of lurid skimpy golden dress, carved pieces and short skirts that still exposed one leg, which was also adorned with shining fragments.

Worn by some of the assembled females, a headpiece with several needle-like fixtures sticking out. Others carried a multicolored feather boa.

Males wore brown golden-lined tunics with its shoulders and arms made of a more ridged material, finished with dark green trousers; and of course, all with cut-outs for their wings.

They sampled the union foods with which a table was laden. For such a feast there was wild bovidae and ovis marinated in wine and baked in an out-of-door oven in the nuptial courtyard. There were some of the local wines, and the special wedding pastries.

Minor-key wailing accompanied trumpets as they blew, the dancing ceased, privacy curtains withdrew, and the procession began. Voices soon rose in song.

One by one the hopeful postured down the catwalk like the perfect dolls they had been groomed to be for the eager bridegrooms ogling from the audience around in the U-shaped voting pit. Each dressed in their elaborately jeweled gown. Ballots were cast, tallies made, decisions quickly made.

Destiny was soon to be met by the prepared. Father Warner drew his slip, he declared it was his seventy-seventh time participating in the pageant. Males took their slips before everyone opened them. The crowd looked around wondering which pullet was "won" to which male.

A set of young males smiled as they held their numbered slips above their heads for everyone to see, splaying their wings to show the endowment of wingspan. Several of the pullets saw their matching number on the slips, the grateful smiled and chirped; the others frowned, capitulating to the inevitability of chance.

Seminarian Graves opened his and the matching pullet sighed. When all had been revealed, First Father then instructed the crowd to "finish quickly" as they moved the partnered toward privy chambers.

First Father, dressed in a red gown with a large collar, pointed shoulder pads, and gold lining and trim all over, with regal symbols sewed onto the front and back, called for everyone's attention, and then began to read the ceremonial vow qualifiers aloud for all to hear. His expansive wings tucked in along his thin frame.

"Our first tiercel is Aeyuph Sloyab, son of Sloyab Arkhav," he announced, his high-pitched screech echoing off the hall's vaulted ceiling. "An authority in in both poems and literature, innately humble, unrivaled and outstanding abilities, currently serving the Coclaas Rockery, where his grand ambition is to be initiated. He is to be mated with formel Ruvator Wixillian, daughter of Wixillian Skaforb. The two of them have the perfect combination of hatching dates and were especially granted marriage by this Nepantla Selection."

And so, the announcements for each and every Nepantleras was made, until the very last. The elder scribe nodded to each before making his next statements.

"You will each be blessed with much good fortune," his eyes gleamed with pride. "You will be in love for hundreds of years. Being granted a pair of connected phoenix-designed gold ladles. Spouses you are now. Partake in millet."

Handmaidens at station-keeping along the room's peripheral now moved into action. Each holding a bowl brimming with small-seeds from grasses.

One by one each betrothed placed a seed within their beaks and swallowed. The attendants retreated when the ritual was finished. Many of the maids wore ornate outfits with a towering headdress fixed with fabric streaming down, with the chief maid wearing a gold and green dress worn with a large headpiece fastened with colored streamers.

"Drink the broth," instructed the elder.

Another set of servers appeared with another set of bowls; these were filled with a yellowish liquid.

Each of the Nepantleras supped from a proffered basin. When the action was complete, the acolytes moved into the shadows.

"Savor the sauces."

This time both sets of attendants emerged with trays holding several different colored small serving bowls. Each of the tiercels and formels followed each other in taking a sip from the offered variety of liquids. When the servers retreated, the elder nodded pleased.

"Comestible rites complete," he said. "Share the nuptial cup."

In this phase a specially designed cup was given to each of the couples. It was more of a large spoon, tethered by the handle to the other by a silken thread with an ornamental bell sewn between. The couples' synchronized drinking issued a harmonious chiming sound in reaction to the act of lifting the spoon cups to their beaks and drinking the nectar held within each porcelain depression. An odd musical accompaniment to the gesture.

"Kowtow to your progenitrix and progenitress," the elder directed the couples.

In a well-rehearsed movement, as one, the grouping of Nepantleras faced their watching genitors and genuflected as rehearsed respectfully in their direction. Matrons wore a ridged black dress fitted with gloves and ornate spiked shoulder pads, and a much larger black version of the female guests' headdresses.

Patrons were fitted in ceremonial black leather fixed with golden trim, as well as being worn with a variant of the domed elder helmet but with a large flock crest fixed on the front as well as the top of the suit being fitted with pointed shoulder pads and, like the matrons, high-heeled boots worn.

Parental wings fluttered in approval. When all had risen, they turned back to face the elder of the proceedings for the anticipated closure of the ceremony.

"Enter the roosting chamber," he said.

The assembled began to move, each to their own respective destination. One pullet screamed that it wasn't fair as an older male she had been united with descended upon her from a hovering stance.

## CHAPTER FIVE:

"Harec, are you willing to leave with me?"

Roooccy Grun leaned on the thatched roofing of his congregational nesting yurt donning a torso harness fashioned with four shoulder strap buckles framing his well-developed chest and one collar buckle to hold it firmly in place, the black leather construction matched his triangular cut loincloth.

He looked intently into the dark eyes of his true love, Harec Zurir. She was a timid female, never one to upset the norms, but now she had been mated to someone she abhorred and refused to continue in a life unfulfilled. Her desire was evident as she met Roooccy's stare.

"To where?" she asked. She had cast-off her nepantla gown and now simply wore a form-fitting leather lavender pentagram harness strapped top that caged her chest and body. A delicate fringe detail skirted around her pelvic girdle. Her wings and tail feathers were free from restraint.

"The ends of the world," Roooccy replied, patting his satchel slung from his left shoulder over to his right hip.

Unfastening its burlap flap revealed tightly packed contents such as two canteens of water, a medical triage kit, and small travel-sized transparent pouches filled with seeds, lean trimmed meat that had been cut into strips and dehydrated to prevent spoilage, as well as dried pieces of fruit.

Refastening the overlap, he cooed, "No matter where. I love you, Harec. I will not let you suffer. Your matron may not thought me suitable for you, but know that no one can stop us from being together. Harec, do not worry."

"I've always wanted to explore below."
"You mean the land under the clouds?"
Harec nodded enthusiastically.

With conviction, Roooccy extended his closest hand to her. "Then let's go!" he said. "I know of a place no one will think to search for us."

Hand in hand the two swooped up high above the cityscape. It resembled so many chess pieces seen from above in miniature.

Urban life took on a whole new dimension when seen from overhead. Straight avenues shot out like the points of a star; skyscrapers felt even more vertiginous. Lights glittered as far as their eyes could see from on-high.

Like an artist's palette, Coventry's panoramic promenade views offered up a mixture of warm and cool shades amid odd shapes jutting upward like monstrous pins in a cushion.

With glee they tucked in their arms and legs as they narrowed their wings while expanding their tail feathers, they dove over the elevated city's sloping ramparts. Beneath and between them and the planetary surface lay thousands of miles of mostly nothing. Minute muscular movements adjusted their descent attitude until they were rocketing along head-downward and in parallel.

It was the silence that struck Roooccy. Free-falling in emptiness, he noticed there was no sound except the familiar pounding of his own heart and the bellows that were his lungs. Llel was rushing toward them at incredible speed, its calico landscape threatening to rise and smash them flat. Falling back on basic breathing exercises he had learned in catechesis, he fought to regulate his respiration and heart rate. Despite his best efforts they remained high.

The three Glaseran suns floated high in the sky. Both Llelans were plummeting toward the surface far too fast to make out any details revealed by the heliotrope light. Cloud banks of immense opaque density whisked passed them at incredible speeds.

Vapor seemed to vanish as they penetrated through layers of heavy overcast. Descending at numbing velocity toward the planet below, Roooccy knew that just as they'd had one chance to hit a stop point, they would have one chance to land safely.

Harec let out a screech of delight just as she pulled back and cupped her wings, splayed her tail feathers – both acting as a chute. Roooccy immediately followed suit at almost the exact same time. Untucking their legs, both reached them out for solidity as their speed was greatly reduced. They came to land and then stand at the beginning of a dirt path that led east and west.

In both directions, parched brown hills stretched to the horizons. The land was far too unpredictable for any powered vehicle. High above and away the vapory silhouette of Coventry hung like a lunar mirage.

"Where are we?" asked Harec.

Roooccy pointed and answered, "Beyond the hills to the west lie the Forgotten Marshlands, hundreds of miles of treacherous swamp." He gestured in the opposite direction, adding, "To the east stand the mysterious Murk Mountains. There are hundreds of caves carved into those hills, connected by a labyrinth of tunnels. So myths tell."

"So, do we go east?" Harec questioned. "Or go west?"

"Or do we wait to see if anything interesting happens right where we are standing?" Roooccy smiled.

"Let's go east," Harec suggested. "If you are certain no one will search for us here, being out in the open will leave us susceptible to being found."

Roooccy bowed and gestured for her to lead the way.

The path beneath their sandals turned to hard, red clay. The first hill was farther away than it appeared. They walked for nearly an hour until they came upon a gleaming object lying on the baked ground. It appeared to be a jewel-laden, round shield. Perhaps it was dropped by a previous wanderer in the badlands. Its silver coat shone like new. Rubies and emeralds formed a circle around its edge.

"Should I take it?" Roooccy asked.

"Yes," Harec said. "It's beautiful. We may need it."

"There is something odd about the shield," Roooccy replied, pulling back an outreaching arm. "If it has been lying under the hot suns for a while, why is the silver still so shiny?"

They continued east along the path, leaving it behind. The path took them to the top of the first low hill. To the east, they saw a taller hill. It contained three small caves. To the north, they saw what appeared to be a lake.

"Water?" Harec asked.

"No," Roooccy corrected. "There is only one lake in these lands, and it is many miles from here. Let's continue east."

They climbed the tall hill and found themselves standing near the entrances to the three caves. The first appeared dark and empty. An odd shaped silhouette moved in the arc of the opening to the second. The third cave seemed to have light flickering inside.

"Is that some sort of six-legged animal pacing the second entrance?" Harec observed. "Which cave do we enter?"

"Let's follow the light," Roooccy said, moving forward.

Together they walked over to see what illumination shone near the entrance. They were astonished when they looked down at the ground near the mouth of the cave and saw jewels. The light they saw was sunlight flickering off emeralds and rubies, which lay scattered about the entrance.

"Treasure?" Harec inquired. "If so, how did it come to be scattered on the ground like this?"

They stood and stared at the jewels. Their beauty hypnotized them.

"We must decide our next move," Roooccy said. "Do we pick up the jewels and stow them on ourselves? Or leave the jewels where they lie and explore the cave?"

"As tempting as these jewels are," Harec told him. "They may have been left here as a trap. I'd rather explore the cave first."

Nodding, Roooccy led the way into a large chamber. A smoldering fire told them that someone lived there. They saw animal bones and piles of cloth. The chamber led north into a long tunnel. It was aglow with phosphorescent fungi embedded in the rough-hewn walls.

Together, they followed the tunnel for hours. It was silent and empty. There were no jewels lying about.

"I am beginning to wonder if we should turn back," Roooccy said.

"We have come this far, let's follow the tunnel to its end," Harec smiled.

The adventure of it all was exciting. And, so far, their escape from Coventry had gone unnoticed, they had no pursuers.

They continued, pausing from time to time to rest. Eating and drinking from Roooccy's satchel rations. Finally, they saw daylight. They stepped out of the tunnel. Before them stood an ancient stone castle. It was now crumbling ruins. It was obvious that the castle had not been occupied for several generations.

"Let's explore," Harec giggled, taking flight and hovering low to the ground as she disappeared into the collapsing rubble of stone and mortar.

Roooccy followed close behind. They explored the dusty chambers carefully. Each still seemed to echo with the ghosts of the dignitaries who lived there, the wars fought on the grounds, and the opulence once contained. A stronghold constructed with twenty-eight bedrooms, an outer hall, an inner hall, two smoke rooms, a dining room, a drawing room, a billiards room, an oak study, and a range of accommodations for servants. The air was fetid, the structure was deadly still. That was until, in an assembly room that may have served as a library, they found a tattered scroll in a corner.

Harec brushed away decades of cobwebs and dust and unrolled the scroll. In ancient Llelan, it read a long column of edicts, but none as ominous as the last line:

`Beware the trove chest in the main dungeon.`

"There's a treasure chest in the main dungeon?" Roooccy shouted in amazement. "This is becoming quite the adventure for us both."

"Do we ignore the warning of the scroll and open the chest?" Harec smiled, childishly inquisitive.

"Or do we obey the words of the scroll and continue to search elsewhere in the castle?" Roooccy countered.

Harec nodded, saying, "Have you noticed that ever since we've landed and begun to explore, this land is fraught with pitfalls and temptation?"

"Yes. It is as if the very land conspires against us."

Rolling the scroll, Harec returned it to where it had been originally discovered. "Let's heed the scroll," she said. "And stay away from dungeons and treasure chests."

"Besides," Roooccy smiled. "There is so much more of this fortress to explore."

A corridor took them to ruins containing the remains of a banquet hall, a watch tower, and a dry harbor. Exploring the grounds, they walked through towers and a courtyard square overrun by the surrounding forest.

Once a grand pillar of excess; now, it lay in ruin. A promenade led down to a tunnel which grew wider, then narrower, but they saw no sign of life, no sign that anyone ever used the tunnel for any purpose. Finally, they saw daylight again.

The tunnel ended just up ahead. Happily, they rushed to the opening. They discovered that the subterranean passage had led them right back to the spot where their journey had begun.

"We've come full circle!" exclaimed Harec. "So much for heading east."

"Would you prefer going west toward the marshland?"

"You did promise me that we could go anywhere in the world," Harec laughed.

They began walking toward the west, following a narrow path carved out of the hard, yellow ground. The three suns of Glaser were high in the sky. It was the hottest time of day. Both Llelans ignored the heat and their thirst, conserving their provision portions. The footway curved to the northeast and they followed it, their eyes alert to any danger.

"We dare not take flight," Roooccy warned. "We would be spotted from Coventry."

Harec nodded and touched his nearest arm with endearment. "I know. Besides, I am enjoying the walking."

Roooccy eyed the deceiving circle of the planet's primary sun above, put his head down and into the wind. It had changed direction four, maybe five times since they had begun the hike. He had been correct about the deceptiveness of the land---and that included distance. It felt as if they had been walking for years without drawing any nearer to their objective.

Eventually the sloping ground leveled out and the easterly mountains sank beneath the horizon behind. Gravel and rock gave way to a broad, flat plain of moss and fine, soft stone. Only scattered monoliths of black basalt broke the gently rolling plateau, volcanic plugs---the mummified hearts of long-eroded fire-spitters. Fortunately, the cloud-laden sky cut much of the daytime heat, or they would have been broiled quite thoroughly.

The dry air was suddenly disturbed by a loud bellowing. A low-pitched roar that chilled the two Llelans to their skeletal cores. The cry ricocheted across the entire valley, distressed sound rebounding from one granite rock to igneous mountain slope to a basalt formation.

"What or who is that?" asked Harec, almost crouching in fright.

The noise faded, most likely lost in the rush of wind and occasional lightning. But it was heard by one whose ears were far more sensitive than those of others.

Roooccy was suddenly alert, cocked his head, listening. It came again, and he pointed toward the desert flatlands. In the distance, two imposing shadows could be see rippling in the heat distortion waves.

The earth was inhabited by giants. The behemoths faced each other as if two players in a caged match. Muscle on muscle, no-holds bar. No referee to stop the fight.

"A desert scorpion," Roooccy identified. "And, a desert centipede."

Two creatures known to be a menace to many creatures, especially each other. To survive in a hostile habitat a resident had to be made of tough construction and none was tougher than the desert scorpion and its superb weaponry. From its stinger at the base of its tail that had quite a potent venom to its modified palps' pinchers, huge enough to grab prey in a vice-like grip. Evolved mouthparts also had pinchers to mash up fresh meat and shovel it in.

Not all opponents were obliging.

An effective arthropod killer, the gargantuan desert centipede was one of the speediest on the bug world fight card. Three hundred and fifty-four segmented sharp-tipped spiked legs were fast and deadly, allowing it to traverse any terrain: soil, rocks, tree trunks or even grass.

At top speed, only three or four legs supported the entire body making it resemble a venomous hovercraft---each leg slightly longer than the one in front of it. At its front end were two vicious venom claws whose sole purpose was to inject toxins that ravaged a victim's major organs. In parallel to a scorpion's food, the centipede could finish off a bite with a lethal injection or rip the prey apart. A biological all-purpose field knife.

In the heat of the new day, each titan faced their nightmare other. The scorpion not adept at mobility in the vast scheme of things when compared to the freight-train of a centipede. On the rocky desert floor, the two apex predators went head-to-head. Size, speed, and tactics mattered. Both had the fight skills to finish each other off.

Another loud warble came as the centipede sized up the scorpion with its antennae. It tried a direct hit but there was no avoiding the pinchers. The scorpion snatched at the centipede with a huge claw. It stepped nimbly aside, fended off a strike of a looming tail, and swung its venom tusks.

The monstrous predaceous arthropod continued to press in. Though the scorpion held it off, it could not gain an advantage. It bared its fangs and roared defiantly, challenging the centipede. It outstretched its forearms and claws, daring the other to get closer. Its tail lashed the air. It had not come this far to shrink from the battle; it was hungry too. The multiple-legged arthropod was prey, dangerous prey but prey regardless. It had to be succumbed.

Together, they promenaded in a circle in a deadly imitation of a dance. Hatred raged in pitch-black eyes as a mutual screech strident for revenge trumpeted.

Backing off, the centipede attacked again. Its assault was enough to stagger even the mighty clawed leviathan. In reflex, the scorpion screamed and tried to retreat and run. To no avail, the centipede had it by its tail in its teeth. Strong enough to pull the maneuver off successfully.

The centipede held on to the scorpion's tail like a vice, biting it fearlessly, and cutting off its opponent's main defense weapon. Having immobilize the tail, the stinger was rendered useless, leaving only claws to defend. The scorpion pivoted and snapped at the centipede.

Locked in combat, the monsters rolled across the clearing, grinding landmark rock formations into dust. Their growls and screeches were matched by the rumble of disintegrating basalt plateaus, eroded towering sandstone buttes, and ancient superficial bedrock deposits.

The ground shook throughout the valley bowl. Waves of tremendous displaced air rushed outward in a concentric, expanding bubble with each flip and collapse the two beasts took. Recoiling noise of the fight was deafening.

The wrestling match produced thunderous 'booms' and temblors with each body-slam. The wind force of the concussions flipped Rooocy and Harec and sent them flying away from the contact zone in a rolling tumble.

Dust and debris flew by on gale force winds.

The howling of distress was enough to make the two recovering lovers shrink back and hide behind some outlying boulders at the horror of it all. It was so raw and wild and mercilessly ferocious. A micro-dust storm had been created in phased granular waves.

The centipede wrapped itself around the struggling scorpion like a coiled spring. Using its entire body and legs, the centipede held its prey in place while it delivered its venom. It sank its fangs through the scorpion's exoskeleton, holding back its muscular pedipalp forearms with six legs of its own. A knockout and submission hold all in one. There was no tapping out in this cage flight.

Desperate and dying, the predatory arachnid roared in pain a keening wail of distress, agony, and fury. The centipede tasted victory. An anguished prolonged high-pitched cry of pain, grief, and anger faded into deadly silence. Within minutes following, it was all over. The prize, to eat your opponent.

The stink that wafted told that death was visiting.

Horrified at the brutality, Roooccy shielded Harec and moved away from the deadly tableau. A brisk breeze sprung up and blew coolingly in their faces. The hard ground soon began to soften in spots.

Small pools of water from some mysterious underground source broke through the dry dirt. In the distance, they could see spots of green vegetation.

"We are approaching the Forgotten Marshlands," Roooccy told Harec. His voice had an odd warning to its pitch.

A short, violent chuff brought them to a halt. Roooccy pointed ahead with a forefinger. "Now what could that be?" he asked.

"Is it thunder?" asked Harec, hopeful that it was not another encounter with a leviathan.

Moving in their direction was what looked like a solid curtain of dark gray reaching laterally across the entire horizon and vertically to the stratosphere. The breeze freshened and beat at them with increasing intensity. Harec glanced questioningly at her beau.

The gray wall moved nearer and was now charging down upon them. The imposing male did not reply. He was staring at the approaching wall. A deluge reached them moments later, a rain of seeming solid intensity.

Using his large wings, Roooccy umbrellaed each one over them, acting as a makeshift canopy, just before they would have been washed away. Harec wrung water from her feathers, smiled radiantly beneath damp eider. "*Real* weather," she mused.

"And more," Roooccy agreed readily, looking out through a gap in his splayed flight feathers. "You would almost think…"

Before he could finish the thought, the rain stopped as abruptly as a curse, to be replaced by a blaze of sunslight. Clouds began to form immediately, but under the attack of the sudden inferno, broad shallow lakes disappeared before their eyes, hissing, all but boiling off the sand. Instantly their damp plumage dehydrated in a flash of steam.

Where vision had been obscured seconds earlier by a solid wall of water, now the landscape shivered and rippled under building heat. Distortion waves added ridges and hills to the surface where none existed. Undeterred, they continued their trek.

The track branched in two directions at this point. One way led northwest into a desert flatland, the other continued northeast into the bog. An arboreal region way beyond.

"We have a directional decision to make yet again," Harec huffed. "Go northwest or northeast? Or get off the path and do some exploring right where we are?"

"So far following the path has led us in circles," Roooccy smiled. "Why not be daring and do some independent exploring. We'll keep the path in view and walk east toward that craggy rock formation." He pointed, she nodded.

A small pool of water stood in front of orange rocks.

As they approached, they saw a reflection of clear green water. To its right, a shiny 'something' lay on the ground.

"More temptation," Harec scoffed.

Roooccy agreed and bent down over the green water and peered into it. A shallow pool, about eight feet deep. Harec climbed to the top of the rocks. She was surprised at how warm the stone felt, and how they were soft to the touch. Near the top of the odd formation she saw a small opening.

"I've found an entrance to another cave!" she shouted down to her companion.

Both stepped cautiously into a large underground chamber. The floor, they were startled to discover, was soft and light-colored, almost pink. Roooccy took another step. The walls of the hollow seemed moist. The ground began to tremble.

"Rooocy!" Harec called out in alarm, already her wings were unfurled, and she was hovering. "I don't think we walked into a cave entrance, we've walked into *something* and this is not a floor at all; it's a tongue!"

"Take flight!" Roooccy called out as he too jumped into a full wingspread.

As if shot from a cannon, the lovers bolted up from the deep, black cavern. Clinging together in midflight, they comforted each other – breathing rapidly as the escaped prey they were. Below them a disgruntled beast roared at its loss.

Coming to rest again on the pulpy earth, they slowly released each other.

"No more adventures," Harec sobbed. "Take me someplace safe."

"Yes," Roooccy reassured. "I will always protect you. No matter where we are or what our situation."

Harec chirped startled when a harsh cry came from above and behind them. Turning, they saw an assembly of rockery guards swooping in for a landing. A shrill keening from above issued from Harec Zurir's spouse in the lead.

## CHAPTER SIX:

"Stop my bride!" Seminarian Nlijaban Talass commanded his posse. A portly elder male, whose soft tissue around his mouth resembled a pouch, dressed in official ministry garb. "Don't hurt her, though!"

Before either Harec or Roooccy could take flight, the band of well-armed security was on them. Restraint batons withdrawn and ready.

Centurions wore helmets equipped with a cone and scope-type sensor planted on top, giving them communication and directional powers. Covering most of their avian bodies was a black leather armor piece, consisting of an adjustable black leather harness with O ring detail. Matching arm bands and collar which had feather-like patterns of gold and black sculpted onto it. Each rockery guard's large powerful wings were exposed, ready for battle.

Admirably, the two lovers fought back. Swift kicks, well-placed jabs, and flogging wing flabs kept the offenders at bay. Talons extended, Roooccy headed for a guard's face. Wings beating at his sides, forelimbs extended.

Harec curled into a tight spinning ball. When she came out of it, it was with both legs tucked tight into her chest. She extended them just in time to meet another guard's midsection. As he tumbled awkwardly from the blow, screaming in pain and rage, the centurion was met from behind by the late arriving Roooccy.

As the sentry collapsed from a well-placed blow to his cervical plexus, another guard had a grip on both of his arms and despite his best efforts, Roooccy could not dislodge him from his back. Harec twisted away from an aggressor, slashing out with a clawed leg.

The guard wrenched aside, and the claw ripped down his exposed front, drawing a little blood along a feathery trail. Straining, the young female managed to fight her way over to her lover's side. Furious at his captor, she turned to rend the sentinel.

Folding her wings, she dropped like a stone toward the restraining birdman. She screamed in triumph as her power dive drove curved talons right through him. The force of the blow had almost knocked Roooccy off his balance---almost.

The security male was far from incapacitated. As Roooccy righted himself, the fallen centurion crawled carefully round and got a grip on Roooccy's wings.

"No!" he shrieked desperately.

Harec moved in for another strike, her attention totally on the battle. She had forgotten everything but that fury. By the time she recognized the shadowy movement from her peripheral vision, it was too late. She too was pinned down. There were only two of them against a superior force. Eventually, both were in restraints and facing the wrath of Talass.

A faint spot appeared above them, resolved into a bloated, unbalanced body centered between a pair of batwings. He banked and glided down to land atop a small outcropping of granite. So much for being in a place where no one would think of searching for them.

"Let go of me!" shouted Harec.

"You brazen abductor!" Roooccy added. "I demand you let us go! Give my love back to me!"

"I did not abduct her!" Talass corrected. "She united with me of her own free will!"

"Nlijaban," Harec screamed. "Even if I die, I did not do anything of my own free will!"

"You call this free will?" Roooccy challenged.

"Whatever *this* is," Talass hissed. "It is our tradition. It is my right! So, what of it? It is her fortune that I like her."

"Good fortune!" Harec struggled against her bindings. Her expression wrinkled into one of pure loathing. "You manipulated my progenitors into this union to free them of over-inflated debt owed."

"Yes, debt owed to me!" Talass reminded. "Your progenitors were indebted to me!"

"And, I was the payment!" Harec spat. "In elder times there was a word for such transactions! A word not used in modern polite society!"

"You are using the fact that you have some power in Coventry," Roooccy accused the other male. "To go oppressing females and acting against reason. You cannot act like this knowing she does not want to be with you! I won't let you do this. This day I will get justice for Harec and me!"

"Very well!" Talass let loose a harsh shriek. "You are quite amazing. I've seen lots of tricks like this before! Do you dare go with me to the magistrate's office?"

"Yes. The magistrate's office will listen to us," Roooccy wiggled his way free of his bindings and stood fully erect before the older, shorter male.

Talass chuckled. "It is not a place to talk logic."

"If the magistrate's office is unreasonable, then is there any place in Coventry that is reasonable?" asked Roooccy.

There was no reply.

Roooccy Grun unruffled his feathering, he smirked. "Let's go!" he demanded, reaching over to Harec and loosening her restraints.

Together the two lovers rose, wings fluttering more violently as they spread wide and beat downward to gain altitude. Beginning a wide circle that brought them into the updrafts sweeping up granite flanks close by, they soared effortlessly higher.

## CHAPTER SEVEN:

All civilized communities had some ways of organizing themselves and regulating their actions of their members. For the people of Llel, the lowest of these tiers was the family group.

The *pater familias* held the most power, his word was law. Above this level were the interactions between neighbors in the community. Their actions governed by customary laws which had arisen organically to deal with common issues like marriage, divorce, property, theft, and murder. Informing these ideas were religious beliefs which were regulated by the priesthood.

The next level up was the ruling class of the patricians. Their laws were delivered in the form of royal decrees to the populous or in the form of rulings passed in judgment of petitioners to the Court. All laws were codified, the common people had a say in the law, but some could change at the whim of the upper classes.

The floating city of Coventry was a hovering metropolis made from high tech materials, sensor networks, new science, and better data all letting architects, designers, and planners work smarter and more precisely. Environmentally sound, fun, and beautiful. It exploded skyward, throwing up rank upon rank of bristling skyscrapers.

The tribunal precinct was set in a park near the financial district, the building spiraled down, into the municipality's core, like an excavation of the city's pre-urban roots. A central courtyard inspired by water gardens; a reminder of the value that ancient Llel culture placed on natural beauty. Around it, a honeycombed glass wall, evoked the cell structure of plants, filled the interior with sunlight.

The main hearing chamber had a lone figure. Postumus Eltea Aetuls was motionless as a statue in the folds of his blue cloak. Above him scripted in a wall-mounted bronze tablet was the infamous motto of his profession.

*"Do not defend liberty, for it is always free, nor defend visible treasures, for all is to be shared; but defend a secret realm."*

The realm was Llel. Under his watchful eyes, lived more than forty thousand descendants of the original settlers, the last great nomads tamed.

"Your majesty is wise!" Talass praised the magistrate as soon as he entered the judiciary room. "Your majesty, please allow me to speak."

The magus was a male of experience and a deep understanding. One known to make decisions based on careful thought and good judgment. A wizen hawk-faced male of elder years, the magistrate perched patiently on his judgment roost observing the pontificating Seminarian.

"Make it brief," the squire crooned. "Everything is ready for the coming-of-age ceremony for the Quan Rockery. I will go there in a few days. I must prepare."

"Lord Justice, the facts are simple, the case very complex. Your judgment is eagerly awaited. I am here to appeal to your sense of honor and tradition!"

"Are you a citizen of this rockery?" asked Aetuls in a monotone that was felt in the very bones of to whom he addressed the question.

Talass nodded.

"And, yet, you show no respect for your law-giver?"

Instantly, Talass gaped and dropped to a knee, bowing his head. Harec and Roooccy bodies having been bent on one knee to the ground as a sign of respect as soon as they had entered.

Satisfied, Aetuls nodded and said, "Now, rise and state your name and your case. Is there something that threatens these institutions?"

"Seminarian Nlijaban Talass," he said, then turned and viciously flapped his wings at the two entwined lovers behind him. "These two! They violate the communal bonding! She is my new bride; he is her long-time lover! I had them apprehended in the Abandoned Below Lands!"

"The lands beneath Coventry?" asked the Lord Justice.

"Yes!"

"Were they found to have any artifacts on their person?"

"No."

"Pardon, Lord Justice," Harec spoke up. "Artifacts?"

A flash frame of images rushed by her mind's memory of a shield, jewels, bright shiny object … *all traps?* She exchanged a look of recognition with Roooccy. His eyes twinkled back at hers knowingly.

"Yes, *mia birdeto*," Aetuls cooed. "Remnants of a long-gone time. Sacred relics not to be touched. To remove them from the revered sites is a crime punishable by pain of imprisonment."

"We found them flying over the Forgotten Marshlands," Talass bellowed. "My bride in the arms of her illegitimate cockerel inamorato!"

"I claim an annulment!" Harec chirped, rising to her full height. "I challenge the twelve tablets!"

Not a constitution per se, rather a compilation of some existing customary laws most of which reflected the rural aspects of the people it governed. Passages for the width of roads, punishment for cattle grazing in another's fields, and even death penalties for singing abusive songs about others all found within the tablets' eclectic laws. Originally carved on wood blanks and set up for public display; eventually updated to bronze for the sake of permanence. For hundreds of years, the citizens of Llel memorized their contents.

"Be quiet!" Talass admonished her. "You have no rights here, no say so in such matters! I have the authority here over you!"

Magistrate Eltea Aetuls had heard and seen enough. With a screech, he flapped his wingspan and landed with a fierce determination within a hands-swipe from the provoking male. "*Enough!* I am the authority here *over all*!" he glared hotly. "Remember your place! This is a tribal assembly court! Now who is making this claim for annulment?"

After a brief bow, the young female said, "I am Harec Zurir, descendent of Zurir J'luff and Sopilax Kolsol."

"You were united with Talass and went willingly to the roosting chamber?"

"Unwillingly united," Harec corrected. "And, I did not return to the roosting chamber!"

"She was with me following the ceremony!" Roooccy spoke up, standing.

"And, you are…?" Aetuls asked patiently.

"Forgive me, Magistrate," Roooccy quickly bowed and rose, answering, "I am Roooccy Grun. Descendant of Grun Visav and Khrelan Syadgin."

"How was this union arranged?" Aetuls asked.

"As payment for debts owed to Nlijaban Talass," Herec said, shameful. "He owns the hatchery of my congregation."

The elder judge's eye-ridge raised in surprise. He seemed to growl. "No consummation was achieved between Harec Zurir and Nlijaban Talass?" Aetuls asked.

Harec respectively bowed her head, shaking it. Roooccy lowered his gaze in kind.

Aetuls shifted his stare toward Talass and exhaled explosively. "Is this true?"

The other male hesitated, shifting his weight nervously.

"Well?!"

"It is true!" Talass confessed. "But, Magistrate…"

"Without consummation of the union then the claim is valid!" Aetuls reminded the brooding male. He turned to look at Roooccy. "And, you, what is your position in this claim?"

"I am ready to sacrifice. I swore I would protect Harec. Until the moment I die," Roooccy professed. "Because I am fearless. No matter where or when, no matter what it takes, I can sacrifice myself to protect her. If I am alive, I will not allow anyone to bully Harec."

Turning squarely to face Talass, he added, "If you dare to touch her, I will kill you! I will not let her stay in this beastly arrangement. And no other male on Llel is going to take her way from me...your Majesty."

"That is for the magistrate to decide," Aetuls reminded, in a solemn tone. Addressing his attending guards, he ordered, "Take the female and hold her. Outstretch her arms."

While Talass cringed, Roooccy stifled the urge to intervene as two centurions complied with the adjudicator's command. Each held Harec with her upper limbs spread well apart before Aetuls.

"My judgment is this," he proclaimed. "Since both males are of-age and proclaim their bonding to the of-age female, it is therefore fair that they should share her." In one swift movement, he unsheathed the nearest guard's sword, saying, "I will cut the female in half…"

Roooccy did not hesitate, he threw himself in front of Harec while Talass shrieked and stepped back into the shadows. Using his body and wings as a shield, Rooocy begged, "Please, spare her. Spare my love. Do not kill her!"

Aetuls halted in mid-swipe, slowly lowering the blade as he met the younger male's eyes. Watched him as Roooccy pleaded for mercy of Harec's life. "Talass can have her!" he sobbed; his wings drooped.

In that moment Talass reasserted himself and grabbed a freed Harec by her wrists, prepared to drag her from the chamber satisfied. "You heard him, Magistrate!" he gloated.

Aetuls nodded, returned the sword to its sheath, and then beckoned Harec to take his outstretched hands. She hesitantly accepted, looking pleadingly into the elder's eyes.

"Gods bless this female," the judge proclaimed loudly. "Her children's children." He leaned forward and nibbled a peck of his beak against her downy cheek. Pulling away, he softened his voice, adding, "Most of all, her true love."

There was stunned pause as Aetuls placed Harec's hands in Roooccy's. It took all of Talass' self-control not to rebut a response.

Roooccy scooped Harec in his broad, strong arms. He cupped his wings to shelter and protect her against any adversary. "Many gratitudes! With all due respect, Magistrate, I am taking her away. Nlijaban Talass is truly not worthy to be her mate."

There was nothing more to be said, Roooccy swung around to exit. Harec was safely ensconced in the safety of his embrace. Even the unsheathing of swords from the judiciary guards was not enough to deter his resolve.

"I will kill those dare to touch me!" he called out. "I cannot stand bullies the most. I must step up for justice."

"How dare you talk such arrogance! If this is how Harec shows appreciation for all that I was about to bestow on her, then forget it! I am not doing the formalities!" Talass chirped.

"I have sanctioned annulment!" Aetuls declared. With a collective sweep of his wings, the guards stepped back and sheathed their weapons. "This is a young male of honor, defending his true mate with his very life. They are free to go!"

As the two lovers took their exit, Roooccy was heard to say, "I will protect you in the future. I won't let anyone hurt you again."

*** 

Talass grumbled as he watched the two lovers fly off together and away from his sphere of influence. Magistrate Aetuls saw the discomfort in his caste familiar. His hardened heart softened, logic asserting itself as a balm.

"Be at ease," the judge soothed, going to stand beside the portly male. "She may be his, however after a time, they may find that having is not so pleasing a thing after all as wanting. It is not sensible, but it is often true."

"High Justice?" Talass looked confused.

"You have become much known by our people, Nlijaban Talass. Known for your quick boredom of 'things'. If I had granted you coupling, she would have your name and your lands," Aetuls explained, "But there would always be Roooccy Grun. Consider this day a great favor to you and all that you own. Remember, there are other Nepantla every season to make part of your harem."

His brow still wrinkled with confusion, the Seminarian nodded, "Gratitude for your wisdom on me this day, Postumus."

"Take my advice," Aetuls added. "Remove all your ties to her congregation. Consider all debts forgiven. They are not worth the greed."

Talass relenting nodded. "Peace be maintained," he capitulated.

"Peace be maintained," the High Elder cocked his head in acknowledgement.

Dismissing all in the assembly room, he fluttered up and back to his preparations for yet another coming-of-age ceremony within his purview in Coventry.

# DISPOSABLE

## CHAPTER ONE:

Ĉielo Station was an ornament contained within a soap bubble in Space just waiting to break. A massive enclosed city located on the Glaser 667-C frontier edge, containing millions of individuals. Delicate yet sturdy transparent geodesic plates interlocked kept the metropolis' internal atmospheric pressure in check with the vacuous vacuum of the Void.

Arcing thoroughfareways looped around and beside and over each other. Each its own district's ecosystem. A place where the rich and powerful had decided to resided, leaving behind the mundane worlds of Un and Para and Llel; finding them too pedestrian and bland.

The station city was an oasis for those that could afford it. A large, rotating space station stocked with mansions, grass, trees, water, and gravity. An orbital torus concept to larger-capacity self-contained poly-paired rings. Large mass aquifer-reservoir and cisterns ballast stabilized the multi-wheel-world's spin, which in turn imparted simulated gravity. Orbiting the star Glaser 667-C like a spinning cellophane ball caught in a breeze, serving as a haven for the wealthy.

A kind of brave new world, for a small fee. A heavenly home to a half-billion ultra-wealthy citizens.

Artificial Domestic Intelligence-4463 or ADI-4463 paused for a moment in its daily routine to take in an inspection of the view outside its master's bay front windows. Designed to interact with organics, it was programmed primarily for etiquette and protocol.

Technological hominid surrogates, including robotic and simulant hominids, had been popularly used in various scenarios, including training, education, and entertainment. For example, healthcare training often involved the use of robotic hominid-like 'manikins' (mannequins) or virtual hominids as stand-ins for patients when training basic skills. In entertainment and education, robotic hominid surrogates were used to simulate real people who were not accessible, such as a celebrity or a historically significant politician.

Surrogates had been realized in different forms, each offering distinct advantages and disadvantages. Such as, robotic hominids had *physicality*, meaning that they occupied space in the environment. If a robotic hominid had articulated body parts and/or a motion platform, it was able to approach an individual, shake a hand, and demonstrate other physical aspects of social interaction.

Perception of surrogate interaction was different according to the type or modality of the simulant; some specific modalities caused people to change their thoughts or behaviors. Age and gender affected behaviors.

The 4463-series had been specifically designed with such considerations. Bipedal and tall with an attractive personality, good sense of clothing, and polished in behavior. Physically handsome, tall, sharp-featured, well built, balanced weight, intelligent. Immortally ageless. Like any appealing being with intellectual touch avoided loose talking, indecency, and rudeness.

A perfect fit for the Losal demesne.

The residence itself one of many large 'mass-produced' dwellings, constructed with high-quality materials and craftsmanship, using a mishmash of architectural symbols to evoke connotations of wealth and taste. A contemporary house and its subsidiary dwellings, nestled in the beautiful Constantin Valley of the Exuah Ring, sat on over one hundred acres of native gardens, a 'private nature reserve'.

Adjacent to manicured topiary lawns a great wilderness area supported a magnificent diversity and abundance of animals from gazelle, impala, kongoni, topi to eland, spending two-thirds of their lives spent grazing. A property surrounded by mature ironwood trees and offered panoramic views across the valley toward the mountains from Diablo's Peak to Constantin Nek, and out over the glistening False Bay. Stylish and eco-friendly, its views hardly blocked by the interlinking and overpassing neighboring ring districts. Prime real estate.

This day was a special day. Rurali Losal was coming home from boarding school on Defan Ring. A typical urban sector that carried twenty-five hundred city blocks looping side by side of urban construction into the station's mesosphere. He'd been away for several years, training to follow in his father's business endeavors' footsteps, to keep the family's wealth intact and forthcoming to future generations. Lineage security. ADI-4463 had not seen the lad since he had embarked to the private, exclusive institution. The very same that his father and his father's-father had attended.

An indentured servant model, ADI-4463 had been in the service of the Losal family for the past three generations. First acquired for the progenitor Siun Losal then passed on into the ownership of his heir, Nuero Losal. And, soon, ADI-4463 calculated, into the permanent residence of young Rurali when he assumed the role of the family's patriarch or *paterfamilias*, the male head of family and household. That day would be soon, relatively speaking.

ADI-4463's affinity for the younger Losal had started soon after his arrival into the family. Helping to raise the toddler into young boyhood and through awkward adolescence, ADI-4463 had grown accustomed to the male's presence within his sphere of guidance.

It had been the boy's au pair, tutor, first friend, and fixer of all scrapes and bruises. It had helped young Rurali to walk and then talk, accelerate in his primary studies and entrance exams, first heartbreak, and coaching in becoming nimble in all his athletic endeavors. Just had it done for Nuero and Sium. That was its primary function. Yet, it mused, it had not become sentimentally attached to the prior Losals, only Rurali. Perhaps that was because it surmised a mutual affinity from the youngest of all the Losal males.

ADI-4463's revere was interrupted by the bell-like voice of the Lady of the Residence, Urista Losal née Selubir. Thanks to modern cosmetic applications, she still retained her curvaceous stature. The form-fitting cut of her lame' inlaid embroidered white pants-suit displayed flatteringly. Her blond short-cut bob of hairstyle swaying as if made of a single follicle as she bounced on higher-than-healthy heels forward.

"He's here, Four-Four!" she exclaimed, dashing across the marble inlaid flooring toward the main entry.

*Clicky-clack, clicky-clack, clack, clack…*

At her approach, the auto-sensor detected both her advance toward and the presence on the other side of the double-panels. The leaves efficiently sliced apart and retracted into their wall pockets with a low hum. Air pressures adjusted, the scent of things growing invaded the atrium.

Dressed in leisure traveling clothes, lightly tanned skin with the color of his palms of hands as the same as the pale, soft skin of his face, of his throat, of the bottom of his forearms, which had not really been exposed to much UV radiation stood Rurali in the opening threshold. Almost a light pink, as glistening and smooth as the underside of a lizard's belly. Private, chaste, unfledged, like a blush on an athlete's face. Sporting a full stock of ginger-colored hair cut in a conservative styling added to his fresh, clean, provincial persona. All told ADI-4463 things about him it never knew to ask.

"Matron!" he exclaimed, embracing her in his well-muscled arms. "It is so good to be back! To see you! Patron?"

"He's virtual today," she explained, pulling away. "But he'll be available for dinner tomorrow and you can greet him in person then."

"Typical," Rurali nodded. "Somethings will never change."

"One day that routine will be yours," Urista chided lovingly, taking him by the hands and leading him fully into the foyer.

That's where ADI-4463 stood in anticipation. The young male did not disappoint.

"Adi!" he shouted in glee. "Is it really you? You're still here?"

"Yes, Master Rurali, where else would I be?"

Rurali laughed, then shrugged. "I forgot, under that cloned-fleshy exterior, you're made out of tungsten or something indestructible! You haven't aged a day…"

"Actually, my construction is…"

"Come here!" Rurali waved off the response and equally hugged the automaton with pure affection. "So happy you are still with us! I had hoped I'd find you still here!"

Suddenly, if only for an instant, ADI-4463 was back to those endless hours after lunch when everybody lounged about in bathing suits inside and outside the house, bodies sprawled everywhere, killing time before someone finally suggested they head down to the built-in ground pool for a swim. Relatives, cousins, friends, friends of friends, colleagues, or just about anyone who cared to knock at the estate's gate and ask if they could use the tennis courts or swimming pool or game room or --- everyone was welcome to lounge and swim and eat and, if they stayed long enough, use the guesthouse.

Urista grew immediately uncomfortable at the affection between the two, how unnatural and garish the behavior. "That's enough," she chastised, physically pulling them away from each other. "No need to be that over-enthused about everything here at the manor. It's just a synthetic lifeform."

Polite indifference, as if she was summarily pushing ADI-4463 away. It stung.

"Matron," Rurali rebuked. "Don't talk that way about Adi! Just because he isn't made of bone and sinewy as we are, does not mean he is not sentient enough to have solicitude."

"*Bahhhh!*" Urista laughed with a dismissive wave. "You always did make more of *it* than *it* is… *it's* just a *thing*! Now, when you were younger, it was only natural that you endowed it with some anthropomorphism. But, you are well past the age to still have any attachment for such an appliance!"

"Matron…"

"It is fine, Master Rurali," ADI-4463 interjected. "I take no offense. I know my place within the household. The same position I have held for over seventy-five years."

"See," Urista insisted. "No offense. Now, let's get your things stowed away into your room and then we can have a proper little chat and get reacquainted over a nice hot pot of tea and some confectionary edibles made fresh for you this morning by Cook!" She looked ADDI-4463 directly in its face-simulant plate and ordered, "You'll see to that, won't you, Four-Four?"

"Yes, Ma'am, immediately!" ADI-4463 bowed. "It *is* nice to have you back in residence with us again, Master Rurali."

"Thank you, Adi! It is good be graduated and back home." Rurali could not resist a gentle patting of a hand on the other's nearest broad shoulder.

ADI-4463 respectfully stepped aside as Lady Urista ushered her son up the grand, curving staircase to the secondary and then eventually the third floor of the dwelling, where a good square footage was devoted to Rurali's personal space.

## **CHAPTER TWO**:

Together, Rurali and ADI-4462 jogged early the next morning---all the way up to the connecting ring's intersection and back. Early the following morning they swam. Then the day after, they jogged again. Rurali liked to run along the shore of False Bay and the promenade when there wasn't a soul about yet and the house seemed a distant mirage.

ADI-4463 enjoyed when their feet were aligned, left with left, and struck the ground at the same time, leaving footprints on the shore that it wished to return to and, in secret, place its foot where his had left a mark.

This alternation of running and swimming was simply Rurali's 'regiment' in graduate school. He always exercised, even when he was sick; he'd exercise in bed if he had to.

As the days became weeks, ADI-4463 noticed there was something at once chilling and off-putting in the sudden distance that crept between them in the most unexpected moments. It was almost as though he was doing it on purpose; feeding ADI-4463 slack, and more slack, and then yanking away any semblance of fellowship that had always seemed to be present. Perhaps it was Lady Urista's influence.

Where before there had always been warmth and affection, now a steely gaze always returned.

A lazy afternoon, during ADI-4463's recharging interval, it multi-tasked by practicing some guitar playing. Finding a secluded spot in the back garden by the swimming pool, it focused on the fingerboard. Albino peacocks strutted and called out in the distance.

A movement in the nearby grass revealed Rurali's presence. He had been lying in the turf. As he propped himself on his elbows and turned toward the melody, ADI-4463 noticed the gaze right away. He had been staring at ADI-4463 while it was strumming the fingerboard, and when it suddenly raised its face to see if he liked what it was playing, there was a cutting, cruel, like a glistening blade instant retracting moment ADI-4463's sight caught. He gave it a bland smile, as though to say, "No use hiding it now."

ADI-4463 had the urge to suddenly stay away from his fellow companion-owner. He must have noticed it was shaken and in an effort to make up to ADI-4463 he began asking questions about the guitar. The automaton was too much on guard to answer him with candor.

"Don't bothering explaining, then," Rurali said. "Just play it again."

"The same one?"

"Yes, the same one."

Quickly becoming disenchanted, Rurali stood up and walked into the living room, leaving the large sectional windows open so that he might hear the guitar playing. He sat at the piano and tapped out the same tune. A separated duet that lasted well into the late afternoon.

## CHAPTER THREE:

The next day they played a one on one match on the tennis court, and during a break, as Rurali was drinking a lemonade, he put his free arm around ADDI-4463 and then gently squeezed his thumb and forefingers into its shoulder in imitation of a friendly hug-massage---the whole gesture very chummy.

ADI-4463 was spellbound. It slacked like a tiny wooden toy whose gimp-legged body collapsed as soon as the mainsprings were touched. Taken aback, Rurali apologized.

"Did I press a 'nerve or something'?" he asked. "I didn't mean to hurt you."

He was mortified if he suspected he had either hurt ADI-4463 or touched it in the wrong way.

"No, Master Rurali," it said. "It did not hurt." It mimicked the face of someone trying very hard, but failing, to smother a grimace of pain.

Rurali was still surprised by his automaton companion's reaction but gave every sign of believing in the pain around it's shoulder.

"After all these years," he said, "of being around you. I still do not know what parts of you are natural and which are artificial. The architects that designed you did an excellent job of simulating flesh and skin. Even your facial expressions are imperceptible from non-synthetic beings."

"Thank you, Master Rurali, I have endeavored…"

"Stop, Adi. Stop referring to me as 'Master'," he sighed. "I have never been comfortable being called your 'master'. It's too close to what a slave would say to their… well…there *master*. I have never thought of you as lesser than me. Rather an equal. You have been a part of my entire life. Yours is the first face I remember seeing in my childhood, not my matrons or my patrons. You are the one that is in my memory at every dance and music recital, every sporting event, every important moment in my life ... so please, can you just all me... Rurali?"

"If you so wish, Mas... Rurali," ADI-4463 correct.

"And, I know that my grandpatron called you Forty-Four and my parents refer to you as Four-Four, but to me, you will always be *my* Adi!"

"I don't mind the different references," the automaton smiled. "As long as I am still called into service. I am 'happy' to be called at all."

Rurali laughed abandonedly, slapping his companion on the upper back. Here was a person who lacked for nothing. ADI-4463 could not understand this feeling. It envied him.

Allowing his sally to fade, Rurali laid back on the nearest plush chaise lounge and closed his eyes. His breathing became shallow, his countenance softened. Speckled shadows from overhead leaves played across this paper-cut profile. After a time, ADI-4463 took notice of the prolonged silence between them.

"Rurali, are you sleeping?" it asked.

Silence.

Then came his reply, almost a sigh, without a single muscle moving in his body. "I was."

"Sorry. Are you dreaming?"

"Yes."

"What about?"

"Private," Rurali replied.

"So, you won't tell me?"

"So, I won't tell you."

ADI-4463 found it amusing when Rurali repeated what it had just said. It made it think of a caress, or of a gesture, which happened to be totally accidental the first time but became intentional the second time and more so yet the third. It reminded ADI-4463 of the way it would make Rurali's bed every morning, first by folding the top sheet over the blanket, then by folding the sheet back again to cover the pillows on top of the blanket, and once more yet when folded the whole thing over the bedspread---back and forth until it knew that tucked in between the multiple fold were tokens of something at once pious and indulgence, like acquiescence in an instant of passion. Ebb and flow.

Silence had become light and unobtrusive in the afternoons.

"So, you won't tell?" it asked once more time.

"I am not telling," Rurali re-phrased his answer.

"Then I will leave you to your ruminations."

Profound silence again. Moments passed...

"This is heaven," Rurali exhaled in pure delight. He remained silent for an hour.

By early evening, friends and neighbors from adjoining properties frequently dropped in. Everyone would gather in the garden and then head out together to the beach below. The Losal estate was the closest to the water of False Bay, and all one needed was to open the gate by the balustrade, take the narrow stairway down the bluff, and were on the rocks.

Ecoku Zadra, one of the girls who six years ago was shorter than Rurali and who that same summer could not leave him alone, had now blossomed into a female who had finally mastered the art of conversation. A lovely young female, a fresh complexioned, smiling face framed with short, dark hair. She was dressed in only a light, semi-transparent shift that revealed an athletic and perfectly formed body. She led Rurali willingly to the beach, he called back to attending ADI-4463, "Please put those data pads away for me. Otherwise my patron will skin me alive!"

The automaton nodded obligingly and set about cleaning up the area on the veranda where the young male had been going over his family's financial statistics as per his elder's request.

"You don't have to be polite to a synthetic, they are disposable appliances," Ecoku giggled. "But speaking of skin, come here." With a fingernail, she gently tried to pull a sliver of peeling skin from his tanned shoulders, which had acquired the light golden hue of a wheat field.

ADI-4463 wished it had done that gesture. It could tell she was quite smitten. Her sister as well. Even the crowd of tennis hangers-on who for weeks had come early every afternoon before heading out to the beach for a late swim would stay much later than usual hoping to catch a quick game with Rurali.

It could not say it was resentful, in fact, ADI-4463 found the affections a strange, small oasis of peace. *What could possibly be wrong with liking someone everyone else liked?* Everyone had fallen for him since his return to the residence, including his first and second cousins as well as his other relatives, who stayed at the manor on weekends and sometimes longer. For something programmed to love spotting defects in everyone else, ADI-4463 derived a certain satisfaction from concealing it's feelings behind it's usual indifference for anyone in a position to outshine it.

"I really wish you would show more respect," Rurali insisted.

"To an automaton?" she looked confused.

ADI-4463 was appreciative of its companion's attempt to overcome the vast gulf separating the classes and bring their worlds together. It was no secret that wealthy industrialists and business magnates and their top employees reigned from high-rise towers and plush palatial country estates, while underground-dwelling cybernetic workers and in-house domestic simulants toiled to operate the 'great machine' of civil divide that powered the spacecity.

A society where disposable beings had been fabricated to maintain a fool's paradise for their creators. Here on Ĉielo Station the only 'living' citizens were the wealthy, eliminating any societal guilt of creating an economy where there could possibly be an argument against social stratification. The artificial had no rights. A society where members had different access to resources and power.

An economic, natural, cultural, religious, interests, and an ideal rift that had no one to complain or protest. Nirvana for the rich and powerful; never a threat to their reign.

"Fine. I'll be nicer to *it*! If that will make you happy. Tell his patron that *I* messed with his data tablets," she smiled back at the veranda table. "See what he says then."

"She is joking, Adi," Rurali corrected. "Never you mind what she says, just please put those tablets in a safe place in the study."

Then the two were off, elbow hooked around elbow almost skipping through the gate, down the stairway, and onto the rocky shore. ADI-4463 heard a high-pitched feminine laugh and cringed.

## CHAPTER FOUR:

A late afternoon, when there was nothing to do in the house, Rurali asked ADI-4463 to climb a ladder with a basket and pick apricots from orchard trees. A small herd of buffalo bathed along the shore of False Bay all the while white triangles of sailing boats punctuated the fluidic horizon on lazy courses to nowhere.

"Only the ones almost blushing with shame," he joked as he held the rungs steady.

ADI-4463 nodded as he freed a bulbous fruit, showing it to the male below it, asking, "Is this one blushing with shame?"

"No," he called back, "that one is too young still, youth has no shame, and shame comes with age."

ADI-4463 embedded the memory of Rurali standing at the base of the wooden ladder in his red swim shorts, espadrilles, billowy shirt, smiling, making it take forever to pick the ripest apricots. Somehow wondering if the young male enjoyed the sight of the hominid simulant form equally dressed casually in blue swim shorts standing above him.

ADI-4463 knew that its designers had molded a form that would be pleasing to the hominid eye, making it tall and handsome. It's daily dress was of modern styling being brief and semi-transparent, scarcely hiding it's lithe and well-proportioned physique. Despite it's chronological age, it still could pass for twenty-something. *Was this the sight of it that Rurali was enjoying seeing from a different perspective?*

Touching the apricots was like touching him. He would never know. He seemed to know more about apricots than he did on his effect on ADI-4463 of late.

"Did you know that our apricots are larger, fleshier, juicer than most apricots in the region?" Rurali asked. "I am fascinated by the grafts, especially when I discovered that the gardener spent hours sharing everything he knew about them with anyone who cares to ask."

"It might surprise you to know," ADI-4463 replied, "that I know more about all manner of foods, cheeses, and wines than all the residents of this household. Even our beloved Cook is wowed and does, on occasion, defer to my opinion."

"Oh really?" Rurali teased.

*"Do you think I should lightly fry the pasta with either onions or sage?"* a perfect imitation of the food preparation automaton issued from ADI-4463's vocal processor.

Rurali was impressed. "Perfect impersonation! Do another!"

*"Doesn't it taste too lemony now? I ruined it, didn't I?"* ADI-4463 went on without prompting, sensing it would be wanted. *"I should have added an extra egg---it's not holding! I should use the new blender, or should I stick to the old mortar and pestle?"*

"Brilliant!"

"Like all food preparer units," ADI-4463 explained, "Cook knows everything there is to know about food but cannot hold a knife and fork properly. Gourmet aristocrat programming with plebian manners."

Rurali laughed out loud again, bending backwards with pure delight. He stopped when he heard his name being called from the veranda. It was

Ecoku, she stood leaning on the balustrade waving his way. Her causal dress rippling in the breeze.

Their moment was spoiled.

Rurali rushed up from the orchard garden to meet her. They embraced.

ADI-4463 descended the ladder, wicker basket hooked in one elbow. Without pause to examine what was transpiring between the two hominids, it proceeded into the kitchen to process the apricots for storage and use later.

Knowing how much Rurali enjoyed apricot juice, ADI-4463 saved an appropriate amount of the fruit to squeeze into a fine, pulpy concoction. Pouring the drink into two large glasses, aiming straws into each as if they were darts, and proceeded toward the patio.

On it's way, ADI-4463 stepped into the living room and took out the large picture book of painting reproductions. It placed the tome on a tiny stool by the book shelving's ladder. It would not show him the book. It would just leave it there. He'd know.

On the patio, Urista Losal was having tea with two sisters who had come all the way from Venan Ring to play bridge. The fourth player arrived, and they began dealing the deck. In the back of the dwelling, from the garage area, ADI-4463 could hear the bionic driver discussing soccer players with Nuero Losal.

ADI-4463 brought the filled drinking glasses to the far end of the patio where Rurali and Ecoku had pulled out chaise lounges and faced them to the long balustrade to enjoy the last half hour of full sun. Rurali liked to sit and watch the waning day spread itself out into pre-dusk light. ADI-4463 often shared such moments with him. Usually it was after they went for a late afternoon swim, but it was good to read then as well.

Being as unobtrusive as possible, ADI-4463 placed the glasses on the shared side table and quietly slipped away, into the house to prepare Rurali's bed for sleeping. The gesture may have slipped the male's attention, but not Ecoku's.

"It always seems to anticipate your every need," she smirked.

"What?"

She gestured at the two glasses on the side table between them.

"Oh? Apricot juice!" Rurali exclaimed in delight. "Who...? Did Adi do this?"

"Who else?" Ecoku seemed to hiss. "Your *too* personal valet. It's always underfoot!"

"What are you talking about?" Rurali asked, totally clueless to where her ire was being generated. "Don't tell me you are *jealous* of Adi!"

No response. She was looking away from the setting sun.

"You *like* him, don't you?" she eventually asked.

"Yes," he said.

"*It* likes you too---more than you do, I think."

"Is this your impression?"

"No, it's everyone's."

Rurali shrugged his shoulders and took a sip of the juice. The apricot pulp was fleshy and the liquid smooth and earthy. Just the way he liked it. Thoughts gripped him. *What if, right now, among some of the folk he had befriended, or among all those people who clamored to invite him for dinner, he was to let out, or just hint at, what was happening between him and his domestic AI? In his place, would he have been able to keep a lid on such a secret? No.*

"I could care less," he said. "Adi has always been in my life, will always be in my life, and if anyone cannot accept that, then ... well... they don't need to be in my life."

Ecoku remained silent.

"Are you pissed at me?" he asked of her.

No answer.

"You are pissed?"

No answer

"So, you are pissed."

No answer.

"So why do you stick around?"

He looked at her, one adult to another.

"You know exactly why," she growled, folding her arms across her abdomen.

Silence. He shook his head.

The air was suddenly thick and muggy, as if the Ring had been awash in a rainstorm that had come and gone and relieved none of the dampness. With dusk scarcely an hour away, the far off promenade streetlights glistened through dense halos, while the lighted storefronts of exclusive boutiques seemed doused in gleaming colors of their own invention. Dampness clung to every forehead and every face. The four card players began fanning themselves in complaint to the change in climate.

"I'm hungry," Rurali announced, standing up from the chaise lounge.

"Isn't it too early for dinner?" Urista asked from her ear-shot position on the patio with the two sisters and the fourth person playing cards.

"It's past eight, Matron."

"So it is," chimed the three female card players in unison.

"Time flees," one sister joked, laying her cards down.

"Yes, we've got our own dinners to attend," said the other sister.

The fourth female nodded and began to gather her personal effects.

Urista escorted her friends to their transports, knowing they had to leave. Dinner was pushed back by another ten minutes so the utilitarian chef could accommodate the early request for dining. Urista sat next to her son. Ecoku quietly left the residence without as much as a 'good-bye'; her mind roiling with confused mental reasoning.

Nuero Losal's seat was empty. Urista complained that he should at least have let her know he wasn't coming for dinner. If he was late for dinner, he would not eat with them. But if he was late that meant he was having dinner elsewhere. Urista did not want her spouse to have dinner anywhere but with their small family tonight.

"It might be the boat's fault, again," Rurali conjectured.

"That boat should be totally dismantled," Urista joked. She clamped down on her anxiety. Showing that she did not care. Staying calm. She didn't want to hurt again. But that moment in what seemed like bliss now when sitting at the dining table with her son, her connection to her wedded spouse kept them apart as if by light-years. She did not even notice that the first course of the meal had been plated.

Following the final course, Urista excused herself, feigning a dull headache and retired to the master bedroom. Rurali was too amped up from the day's journey to go to sleep. After wandering about the household, idly ruminating in the study, on the patio, even the living room; spying an opened book on art, he found ADI-4463 waiting patiently bedside for him, sheets and blanket pulled back, pillows fluffed in anticipation.

"Do you mind if we just went for a walk?" Rurali asked of it.

"Whatever you wish," ADI-4463 replied, in typical accommodating fashion.

The automaton wanted the walk to never end. The silent and deserted alley was altogether murky, and its ancient, pockmarked cobblestones glistened in the damp air, as though an amphora's contents had been spilled before disappearing underground. Everyone had left the Ring Promenade. The emptied gallery, which had seen too many and seen them all, now belonged to the two of them, alone. If only for one night, in the perfect image. The mugginess was not going to break tonight. They could, if they wished, walked in circles and no one would have known, and none would have minded.

"I noticed the book on painting reproductions in the living room," Rurali smiled. "I know it was you who put it out for me. I appreciate what you did."

"I knew you'd enjoy it."

"Gratitude."

They ambled down an emptied labyrinth of sparsely lit streets.

"I wonder how we will move through time," Rurali eventually said. "How time moves through us, how we change and keep changing and come back to the same. One could grow old and never learn a thing but this."

"That is a mortal's life lesson, I presume," ADI-4463 replied.

"Returning home from being away for six years," Rurali confessed, "being here tonight with you seems totally unreal, as though it has happened to an entirely different me."

"Nothing has changed," ADI-4463 reassuringly spoke. "I have not changed. The residence has not changed. Yet nothing ever is the same. All that remains is dreammaking and strange remembrance."

Silence. They sauntered down the dark alley, exactly like two shades in a poem, the younger and the older. It was still very hot and ADI-4463 caught the light from a streetlamp glistening on Rurali's forehead. They made their way deeper into an extremely quiet alley, then through another, as if drawn through the unreal and sticky goblin lanes that seemed to lead to a different, nether realm when entering in a state of stupor and wonderment. The splashing of water was nearby. A marble fountain, like so many found everywhere in the promenade.

Rurali stopped by the large basin and washed his face with the fountain's water. He removed his cap and his ginger hair was all undone. They continued on, returning to another dark, deserted, glistening side alley. Above them was a weak square streetlight mounted to the wall of a tiny old corner building.

"In the original days," Rurali said. "Gas jets would have been used in this place."

He stopped. ADI-4463 stopped. He pressed the automaton against the wall and started to kiss it, his aroused hips pushing into the other's, his arms about to lift it off the ground. ADI-4463's ocular-implants were shut, but it knew he had stopped kissing it to look around them; people could be walking by.

ADI-4463 did not want to look. Let him be the one to worry. Then they kissed again. Pent-up sexual tension released. And, with it's eyes shut, it thought it did hear two voices, old male's voices, grumbling something about taking a good look at 'these two', wondering if in the 'original days you would ever see such a sight.'

ADI-4463 did not want to think about them. It did not worry. If he wasn't worried, it was not worried. ADI-4463 could spend the rest of it's existence as they were now: with him, at night, in the Ring Promenade, oculars shut, one leg coiled around his.

"I see you are excited, too," Rurali laughed, hugging him tightly.

"I am self-aware, sapient, sentient, and anatomically fully functional," the android simulant smiled.

They kissed, groped a little longer. ADI-4463 could have gone forever. But dawn was approaching.

Except for a few transports, the promenade was dead quiet. How wonderful to walk on a muggy pre-morning like this around the gleaming slate cobblestones with someone's arm around you. They left the alley and turned left, and suddenly from nowhere, made out someone strumming a guitar, singing not a modern song, but as they got closer, an old classic tune. It took Rurali a moment to recognize it, ADI-4463 knew immediately.

ADI-4463 looked at him, it wanted one more kiss.

"Tomorrow, let's spend the entire day together," Rurali said.

"Tomorrow is today," ADI-4463 replied.

## CHAPTER FIVE:

A week later, sitting in the living room after lunch having coffee, Nuero Losal brought out a palm-sized tablet. On the small screen were six applications accompanied with the passport identifications of each applicant. He had a perfectly ordinary, if a much unaltered, middle-aged male's face. An older version of his son framed with salty, close-cropped hair.

"Next summer's candidates for internship," he said. "I want your opinion, Rurali, as well as your matron's."

"My successor?" joked Rurali, picking one application above the rest and passing it to his mother.

Nuero instinctively darted a glance in his spouse's direction, then immediately withdrew it. "No. Your intern," he said simply.

"I do not understand," Rurali said baffled.

"Your patron is trying to tell you something," Urista gushed.

"The time has come," Nuero announced. "That you assume your heir-apparent duties to this family."

"What?" Rurali shrugged, dumbfounded.

"And, I step down and assume mine in retirement."

"You want me to take over as CEO?"

Nuero nodded, then said, "You are of-age. This summer is the last of your post-adolescence. I am getting too old to make the right decisions in this modern era. It's time for you to apply all that you've learned while away in preparatory school. Pay back the investment to the family and the company."

"Patron…"

"No need to discuss. The decision has been made. Come next summer, the Company is yours. I'll need at least a season to make the necessary arrangements and transfers, but it is yours."

"Congratulations, Rurali," Urista giggled, hugging her son. "Now your patron and I will retire to the estate's adjacent property and this manor will be inherited by you … and your… spouse."

"Spouse?"

"Yes, your matron and I have noticed that a certain Echo…" Nuero said.

"…Ecoku…"

"… Zadra has taken a liking to you. All reports on her and her family check out. After thinking about it carefully, I have decided she will be a good match for you."

There was a long pause.

"You've decided?" Rurali asked. There was a humoring tone in his voice, concealing his indignation.

"I have," Nuero informed him.

"I would have thought it quite important to have consulted me first," Rurali told him pointedly. "It is not only bad manners; it is bad psychology. It is also bad biology. We may not even be compatible."

"I have been into it all very carefully," the patriarch repeated himself blithely. "You are compatible." Nuero looked directly at his son. "You and this Zadra female will be a fascinating intercaste mix—Vordass and Exuah Rings! Your iron intellect typical of our family interbred with her iron will, so typical of hers."

"It's those very qualities which may get in your way," Rurali told his father. "Your monitoring may not be as good as you think, either. Ecoku happens to be very beautiful, but…"

"But left to yourself, you would choose another. I am aware of that, but it is not the mixture I want. I am afraid I cannot sanction it."

"Someone of flesh and blood…" Urista said sarcastically.

"Matron…!"

"Urista. Enough!" Neuro held up a hand to silence her remarks.

"I never understood your un-natural infatuation with that *thing*," she quipped.

"That *thing*, raised me!" Rurali barked. "Became my best friend and companion…"

"I said enough!" Neuro raised his voice. When the two went silent, he went on, saying, "Urista, you have always been threatened by Four-Four, even I never understood your aversion. But, in the manner of Rurali and his mate, I am doing what was done for me. And, as it turned out, my patron's choice turned out just fine."

Urista smiled in a rehearsed gesture. Neuro nodded pleased. Rurali rolled his eyes at the absurdity.

"I am not asking for your blessing on whom I would choose," Rurali remarked sardonically. He suddenly felt as if he was in a preposterous surreal situation, but as in a dream he was unable to do anything about it. "I make my own choices," he added.

"Much less often than you think," Nuero replied deftly.

Rurali shook his head, mouth open to speak but he could not, when he did, he said, "There's just one thing you have overlooked!"

"What have I overlooked?" The rudiments of a frown crossed Neuro's sun-beaten face.

"Ecoku and I are not rabbits. There's something called love," Rurali protested.

"Oh, love. You do not have to explain love to me," Nuero laughed patronizingly. "You'll see." His tone became businesslike. "Now then, your offspring will be…"

"You would call them offspring," Rurali growled. "You couldn't just call them children." He pursed his lips and looked hesitant. "How do I know I can trust you?" he asked finally. "After all, it would appear, I am completely at your mercy."

"This family needs you! You are my only heir. I cannot continue the company business alone. This is your guarantee!" Nuero said.

Rurali still did not look so happy. He placed his hands on his chin, as though deep in thought.

"Now, enough on this subject," Nuero said dismissive. "Select your intern."

Urista had already begun shifting through the electronic files. "This one isn't so bad," she said, pointing to the face of an applicant she had selected.

Open shirt collar, billowy long hair, the dash of a cinematic celebrity unwillingly snapped by a paparazzo. No wonder she had selected him.

## CHAPTER SIX:

As true to plan, the next summer there was a wedding. No expense was spared. Ecoku heeled in blanched silk footwear in a white metallic textured sequin-inlay gown with dwarf orchid accents in her streaming veil. Rurali in a tailor-cut charcoal jacket with black satin facing lapels, buttons, pocket trim, and a satin side stripe down the leg of the color-matching trousers and shoes, complete with starched white shirt and ebon bowtie. Stunning martial archetypes.

The manor's gardens were sculpted into a facsimile of a Norse outdoor cathedral, complete with long stemmed candles aglow in free-standing candelabras spaced evenly apart under topiary-arcing tree boughs and flittering petals resembling falling snow over the altar dais. Light streamed in shattered amber shafts from breaks in the overhead canopy. In the ode to naturale cathedral, guests sat in neat rows of white chairs in anticipation as the bridal walk score resounded throughout the glade from a string-quartet. Parents beamed with pride of accomplishment in their respective places, each dressed to impress the other side of the mulched path. They all stood as the attendants, groom, and bride took their places for the traditional aisle march.

ADI-4463 was there, off in the shadows with the other servants, dressed in its dress suit. It alone stifling a deep sorrow that it shared with only one other in attendance. For a moment their eyes met, both moist, before tradition overtook the moment and the other was gone, lost to the day's festivities and responsibilities. Birds cooed while vows and rings were exchanged. Food was ate, dancing ensued, libations drank following toasts, gifts were received, and then thank you coms were sent.

The honeymoon was spent traveling abroad on the different Ĉieloan Rings, telecoms were sent back and forth as Urista and Nuero set about packing their personal possessions to be transferred to their new residence away from the main manor. A nice five thousand square feet that Urista would have to "fit all of her eight thousand square feet belongings in somehow, someway."

The summer came and went.

Then came the blank years. For ADI-4463 these were the times when it and the rest of the main servicing staff had little to nothing to do. Rurali and Ecoku were constantly traveling in their supportive roles of the family corporation in its many State and National duties, as well as carrying out important work in the areas of public and charitable service and helping to strengthen national unity and stability. It very much reminded ADI-4463 of when Rurali was young and the need to have a resident au pair, Urista and Nuero lived the same lives, been through the same caste training program. A little bit of history repeating. Broken lives on a loaded gun.

The best gift life bestowed on the hominid simulant automaton was to move the divider forward in time. As Rurali and Ecoku settled into their arranged wedded lives, many segments came and faded, some brought joy and sorrow, many threw the automaton's life off course, while others made no different whatsoever, so that ADI-4463, who for so long had loomed like a fulcrum on the scale of life, eventually acquired experiences that either eclipsed or reduce it's time with Rurali to an early signpost, a minor fork in the road, a small fiery voyage from boyhood through adulthood and beyond. Yet life without Rurali was simply unthinkable.

One summer, nine years post-wedding, ADI-4463 answered a long-distance telecom call. "Servant of the Losal residence," it acknowledged. "To whom may I say is calling?"

"Adi," finally a voice came through. It could hear other voices, including children's in the background. No one could say it's name that way. "Adi," Rurali repeated.

"Yes, it is I," ADI-4463 said. "This is you, Rurali?"

The three-quarter holographic representation of the caller coalesced on the telecom projector, shimmering in blue-white brilliance as horizontal distortion lines rippled up and down the vertical avatar showing some disfigurement. He was dressed in a swimsuit. Fine details of face and physique were hard to discern.

"Who else?" he laughed. "Sorry we have been away for so long. But I have good news for you."

"For me?"

"Yes. We're on our way back. We'll be arriving in a week. Can you see to it that the house is ready? You know, open the windows, dust off the chandeliers, fresh sheets on the beds?"

"But that maintenance is constant," ADI-4463 reassured.

Rurali laughed, again. "I know that, silly. I'm joking with you. It will be good to see in the flesh again. It's been awhile."

"Yes. You've been traveling for quite some time."

He spoke about his two boys, who were right now playing with his matron-in-law—one eight, the other six, Arthur and Oliver respectively, both born abroad---and Ecoku. They were in the most beautiful spot on all Ĉielo next to the main manor—being at their secondary home on the Vordass Ring so that Ecoku could be close to her family, somewhat pretending to infer that he was happy because of the place. Rurali's wife. Rurali's sons.

The very reality of him coming back with more than what he left was too real, too sudden, not rehearsed enough for ADI-4463. Avatars over the telecom was one thing, reading news reels on tablets or hearing about their adventures on the info-public address media was one thing, but to see everything and everyone put together in the flesh was something totally and altogether different.

A call off-projector from his patron-in-law in the distance had Rurali speaking to it in endearing words, "I'm all choked up about seeing you," he finally said to it. "I wish I could be with you all the time."

Time made hominids sentimental; well, some cybernetics too. ADI-4463 had lodged Rurali in the permanent past, a pluperfect lover, put that time in suspended animation, and repressed the memories back in the furthest reaches of his neurotronic synapses. Perhaps, in the end, it was because of time that everyone suffered.

They arrived down the tree-lined driveway. Automaton porters unloaded and then carried huge athlete-duffel bags, gift-wrapped boxes, and assorted sizes of luggage from the estate transports.

Ecoku's hips had widened while her breasts had thickened due to childbearing, she donned a simple sundress featuring a bright avian pattern that accentuated her curves while bejeweled sandals *flip-flopped* as she walked; her dark hair had grown long and was in a tightly-wrapped bun. Rurali had aged well---only a hint of salting to his red hair, indistinct lines around his full mouth and sparkling eyes--and sported leather moccasins without socks, flat front chino shorts, and an untucked pique poly-blend short-sleeved colored tunic. His chest full and chiseled, the abdomen still flat and striated, impressions mere shadows in the tunic's weave, his thighs filled the construction of the short pants. Muscles that seemed alive under the skin as they contracted and relaxed with each action of his gait attested to a continued commitment to his exercise regimen.

Each boy had his own same-gender personal au pair holding their respect hands in accompaniment to the stroll to the front door. Both were their father in miniature. The elder boy had eyes of pure mischief and that way of moving that honest people do, with the spark of a child and a smile that went all the way through to his core. His junior sibling held an aire of reserve, yet he wasn't stand-offish, having a friendly face and welcoming body posture. Both ginger-haired and freckled faced. Dressed in classic style with pops of color and bold prints featuring clean colors in a structured silhouette matching their parents styling.

ADI-4463's role had been shifted to butler and it was waiting for them in the opened foyer, helping put their things down in the atrium. What could it expect? A hug, a handshake, a perfunctory greeting? A gesture to remind it just how distant were the paths they'd taken, it would be the measure of loss that would strike it---a loss it did not mind thinking about in the abstract, but one that would hurt when stared at in the face.

"Welcome home," it greeted warmly.

There was no emotional hug this time from Rurali, only a genuine smile and an appreciative nod from the new master of the house, a cold indifference from the new lady, and total unfamiliarity from the serving automated staffers. The two boys just stood there, mouths agape in awe of all things new before them. ADI-4463 understood. It saddened it. The nature of the relationship between Rurali and it had profoundly changed with the introduction of Ecoku into their lives.

"Your rooms are prepared," ADI-4463 said. "Shall I take you each to your respective chambers?"

"No need," Ecoku said flatly. "It is *our* home. We know the way."

"This place is so much larger than the other place," stated Arthur. "I like it!"

Oliver nodded. "Is this where we are to live?"

"Who is he?" asked Arthur pointing to ADI-4463.

A quick, meaningful look exchanged between Rurali and Eucko. She frowned. Turning to her two small male children, she said in an altered, sweetly-high pitched tone, "Now, this is where you shall be living for the rest of your childhoods. Do you want *me* to show you to your own personally prepared bedchambers?"

"Yes, Matron, yes, please!" they chimed in response.

Even though everything had been arranged via telecom already, ADI-4463 remained silent.

"To your rooms, then," Ecoku gleefully announced, leading the way up the grand staircase and around and up to the third landing. The boys in tow, laughing and giggling as they skipped after her.

That left Rurali alone with ADI-4463. It was not eager to go upstairs with him and was relieved to see the Cook and automated housemaid servants shuffle out of the kitchen and greet him as soon as they'd heard voices in the entryway. Their greetings diffused